molly o'malley
and the
leprechaun

molly o'malley
and the
Leprechaun

by
Duane Porter

cover art
by
Karen Porter

Buried Treasure Publishing— Blue Springs

Molly O'Malley and the Leprechaun

First edition 2007

Cover design © 2007 by Karen Porter.
Interior illustrations by Karen Porter and Duane Porter.

Aillwee Cave bear logo used by permission of Aillwee Cave, Ireland.

Library of Congress Control Number 2007908052

Publisher's Cataloging-In-Publication Data
(Prepared by The Donohue Group, Inc.)

Porter, Duane.
    Molly O'Malley and the leprechaun / by Duane Porter ; cover art by Karen Porter. – 1st ed.

    p. : ill. ; cm. – (Molly O'Malley ; 1)

    Summary: An eleven-year-old girl from Chicago is sent to stay with her aunt in Ireland where she encounters a leprechaun.
    ISBN-13: 978-0-9800993-0-0
    ISBN-10: 0-9800993-0-7

1. Leprechauns–Juvenile fiction. 2. Ireland–Juvenile fiction. 3. Dragons–Juvenile fiction. 4. Wishes–Juvenile fiction. 5. Leprechauns–Fiction. 6. Ireland–Fiction. 7. Dragons–Fiction. 8. Wishes–Fiction. I. Porter, Karen. II. Title.

PZ7.P67 Mol 2007
[Fic]   2007908052

Printed by United Graphics Incorporated
2916 Marshall Ave.
P.O. Box 559
Mattoon, IL 61938-0559
www.unitedgraphicsinc.com

Published by Buried Treasure Publishing
Blue Springs MO 64015
www.buriedtreasurepublishing.com

To Susan, whose love for all things Irish
continues to inspire me.

Acknowledgements

Many people have helped make this book possible. Thanks to Jim and Shirley Roselli, Harry McAleavy and Steve Naughton for their insights on touring Eire.

A special thanks to my editors; Anita Mosley, Beth King, Linda Carrell, the Ladies2Die4 critique group, Cathy Porter and Haluk Oran for their editing and general comments on the story.

I'm sure you'll agree that the fantastic cover by my daughter, Karen, certainly deserves a special mention.

Finally, thank you to our hosts at the Rockyview Farmhouse in Murroogh, Ireland: Ita and Noel Walsh, and their daughter Isabelle. It was grand reading stories from the manuscript together and talking about what was truly Irish and what was not.

contents

chapter one

The Longest Summer

Molly O'Malley heaved a deep sigh as she dumped her books into her backpack. Finally *this* day was almost over. It was so hard to concentrate lately, with everything going on at home.

At least Mr. Henderson wasn't too boring in science class today. It was kind of cool learning about plants that grew in the tundra, clinging to life above the permafrost where the soil never thawed. Molly identified with those hardy plants, surviving in a cold, unfriendly environment.

I live in the tundra. She shook her head just thinking about it, making her shoulder-length red hair bounce. Why did *everything* have to be so hard in 6th grade?

The other kids were starting to put their things away, too. Molly spotted Will Baxter slipping into the classroom to hand a note to Mr. Henderson. Will was one of the honors students who got to deliver messages to teachers from the office. Kind of late in the day, Molly thought.

Mr. Henderson read the note and looked up. His eyes locked on Molly's.

Molly froze. Oh, no! The note's for me? What did I do? She looked away as Mr. Henderson managed a brief smile.

The last bell rang. Molly put her head down and slid toward the door as quickly as she could. But Mr. Henderson was already there, waiting. "Molly, would you stay for a minute, please?"

She nodded and sat back down as her classmates stampeded into the hallway. When they were gone, Mr. Henderson walked over to her. "You need to go directly to the office and see Mrs. Watson before you leave today."

"Mrs. Watson? The counselor? But I didn't do anything, Mr. Henderson!"

Mr. Henderson shrugged his shoulders as he smiled. "Molly, I'm not sure what it's about, but this note says that you are to go to Mrs. Watson's office instead of the school bus today. I'm sure there's a good reason for it."

The hallway seemed to stretch on forever as the last of the students darted for the buses. The building was downright spooky without the bustle of 300 kids walking around. Going to the office was something else entirely. Molly was not a frequent visitor there.

She tugged the glass door open and stepped into the office. The secretaries, busy with their final tasks for the day barely looked up as she passed, but Mrs. Watson's door was still open in the back. Molly adjusted her backpack and peered around the corner. "Mrs. Watson?"

A pleasant looking middle-aged woman looked up over her reading glasses. "Come in, Molly. Set your things down, and have a seat over here. How has your day been?"

Molly slumped into the chair, lowering her backpack to the floor beside her. "All right, I guess. Will this take long? I don't want to miss my bus."

Mrs. Watson sighed and took off her glasses. She folded her hands and gave Molly a smile. "Don't worry about the bus today, dear. Other arrangements have been made. Molly, can I talk with you for a bit about what's been going on at home?"

Other arrangements? "I really don't feel like talking about that, Mrs. Watson. I just want to go home." *Liar,* a voice whispered inside her head.

"I understand this is not an easy thing to talk about. You have done a wonderful job in keeping your grades up to at least a B, but some of the teachers have noticed that you seem distracted in class. Sometimes it helps to talk. That's what I'm here for, Molly, to listen to whatever you want to share."

Molly looked down at her sneakers. "Mrs. Watson, there is some stuff going on at home, but it's stuff that happens to everybody. It'll get straightened out."

"Well," said Mrs. Watson, "I certainly hope so. Your father will be here in a few minutes to pick you up."

"My father?!" Molly's head snapped up so fast it made her neck twinge. "He's coming here?"

Mrs. Watson looked sad. "Molly, is there something you want to tell me about your father?"

Molly sat back in her chair, rubbing her neck. "Not much to tell. We don't see him too much. He's always out on sales trips." She leaned forward, her green eyes flashing. "He's coming *here?*"

Mrs. Watson shifted in her chair and straightened a pile of papers on her desk. "Yes, he's coming here. Your teachers have listed all of your assignments for the next two weeks, and Mr. Pratt, the custodian, has retrieved your books from your locker for you. It's a good thing there are only two weeks left in the school term."

Molly stared at the counselor in disbelief. "I'm not coming back to school? Did I get expelled or something?"

"Oh, no, dear, nothing like that! You haven't done anything wrong!" Mrs. Watson's face was a picture of concern. "We just want to make sure you have all the things you need to finish out the school year. We're so close to the end of the term."

"But why am I leaving?"

"Molly, I'm afraid I am going to have to leave that until your father arrives."

"That could be next week," Molly growled under her breath.

Mrs. Watson pressed her lips together tightly and looked at the glowering girl across the desk. The older woman smoothed her perfectly coifed hair and lightly cleared her throat. "Molly, it sounds to me as though your father's business might be causing some problems at home?"

Molly rolled her eyes.

"I take that as a yes?"

"All right, I give in. Yes, my father's business is causing problems. He's away on long trips most of the time. He makes a lot of money, we have everything we want ... "

"Everything except ... ?"

"Everything except him. It's like he only comes home to plan the next trip. It's really hard on Mom, she's trying to do everything around the house, grocery shopping, running all of the errands, even car repairs." Molly's eyes narrowed. "By the way, why isn't my mom coming to pick me up?"

A light knock at the door interrupted them. "Come in," Mrs. Watson invited. Framed in the door was a lanky, handsome man with red hair, wearing a slightly disheveled business suit. His tie was loosened about his collar.

"Mrs. Watson? I'm Sean O'Malley. I'm here to pick up Molly." He glanced at Molly with a worried look on his face.

Molly looked at her father as if she had never seen him before — which was almost true. "Dad?" she asked. "What's going on? Where's Mom?"

Sean O'Malley sighed and ran his fingers through his hair. "Your mom's at the hospital, honey. We need to go."

Molly had no idea she could have so many questions. She was even more surprised that she would want to talk to her father. Given the situation, however, there was no choice. Sean O'Malley was the only person who could provide any answers at all. Right now, answers were like a drink of water in the desert.

"Can you talk to me now? We're three blocks away from the school. What's wrong with Mom?"

Molly's father continued to look straight down the road as they approached the freeway. "Your mom is just very tired, that's all. She's near a state of exhaustion, from what Dr. Blake said. She'll need to rest for quite a while to recover completely."

Molly crossed her arms and pressed herself back into the seat. "It's not just being tired, Dad. I know she's tired — of doing everything by *herself* — but she's worried about always *being* by herself! You're never here ... you're always on a business trip in New York or Atlanta or Hong Kong or somewhere!"

"Now, Molly," her dad said, "I haven't been to Hong Kong for at least two years... "

"Ooooh!" Molly threw her hands up in the air. "You're not listening to me! Even when you're home, you don't listen! It's not where you go; it's how much you're gone! Mom misses you! I miss you, although I'm not sure why, since I hardly see you any more! Why do you even bother coming home at all?"

Mr. O'Malley didn't answer as the BMW accelerated onto the freeway. Silence clung to father and daughter like a wet pair of jeans. Several exits passed by the window as Molly fidgeted in her seat.

Tears welled suddenly in her eyes. "Dad, I'm sorry I said that! I'm just ... It's just ... " Uncontrollable sobs shook her small body.

"Molly, Molly, it's all right, dear." Mr. O'Malley blinked a stray tear from his own eye. "It's just that my business is very demanding for me, too. I want to give you and your mother the best I can. You deserve the best. When your mom gets better, we can all take a vacation. Maybe the Bahamas ... "

Molly's sobs softened and she swallowed. "You know, Dad, I don't really enjoy most of the things you buy us. I spend my time helping Mom and worrying about how sad she is all the time. It's like you're trying to buy us off or something. When you get me something nice, each time I look at it, it only reminds me that *you're* not here. Do you know how that makes me feel?" She looked up with her eyes glistening, her breath hissing through clenched teeth.

The turn signal clicked monotonously as they turned onto the exit ramp. A blue hospital sign with an "H" on it pointed to the left, and the sprawling complex of St. Paul's Hospital crawled into sight above the buildings.

St. Paul's, like many hospitals in Chicago, had a proud history dating back to the 1950's. It had been continuously updated with new additions and renovations over the years so that it was impossible now to see the original building. The entrance had been updated about 15 years ago, replacing the bright aluminum trim on the wide automatic doors with a sedate brown that matched the mood of the people coming in.

Molly was glad that hospital rules had relaxed over the years. Now an eleven year old could come in to visit her mother, and the adults didn't seem to worry that the kids would bring the plague in with them. She sighed thinking about it. Why do adults always seem to mess things up that should be simple, and then take forever to fix them? She stole a glance at her dad. *It's not just hospitals that are like that.*

Kate O'Malley had a private room on the east wing. Molly and her dad walked in to find her sleeping, and sat down quietly next to her to wait. Her blonde hair flowed across the pillowcase, framing her face. Even in sleep, her brow was pinched in worry, and Molly felt a pang of fear and anger mixed together as she watched her.

Finally her mother stirred and opened her eyes. A smile stretched over her face as she saw Molly. "Hello, sweetie. How are you doing?" Molly grabbed her hand and tried to manage a smile in return. "Mom, are you all right? What happened? When can you come home?"

Mrs. O'Malley looked over at her husband and the worried look returned. "I don't know, honey. There are some things I have to work out with your father. Pull your chair closer, and let's talk."

"Kate, you need your rest. We don't need to get you upset..." Molly's dad began.

"No! No, Sean, this is important. We need to talk. If you want me to rest, we need to get through this." She turned her blue eyes back to Molly. "You know that we've been under a lot of stress, with your dad being gone so much, and I..." she stopped as tears began to flow down her cheeks.

"Mom..." Molly began.

Her mother shook her head and went on. "It's all right, Molly, it will be fine. Your father and I are going to talk. But the doctor said I'm going to need to rest for a while, weeks at least. Your dad is going to hire in a housekeeper so the house won't fall apart. You know he couldn't manage it on his own."

Molly nodded, blinking back tears. "Don't worry, Mom, I'll be there to help out. I know what to do."

Kate O'Malley looked up at her husband again. "Sean, you need to tell her. I just can't." She squeezed Molly's hand harder and fell back against her pillow. "Tell her."

Molly looked at her parents in turn. "Tell me what?" She looked at her father. "Tell me what, Dad?"

Her father cleared his throat and looked uncomfortably at his wife. "I'm going to have a lot to do that will be difficult for me. I'll do my best— you know I always give it my best, Molly — but I'm not going to be able to handle all this with your mom and my job... and you."

Molly's jaw dropped. "I can't believe this! You're picking your job over me?" She began pacing along the bed, her arms flailing wildly. "All of a sudden I'm just another one of *your* problems?"

"No ... no, Molly, you're not a problem. I just need some time to sort everything out. Your mother and I decided ..."

"Leave me out of this, Sean! This was your idea. I just don't have the strength to fight it any more ..." Kate O'Malley threw her pale hands over her face.

"I decided," amended Mr. O'Malley, "that you should visit my sister Shannon for a few weeks. Maybe the whole summer." He moved to comfort his wife, but she pushed his hands away and began to sob. He slumped into the chair and covered his own face.

Molly looked back and forth at her parents, unable to speak for the moment. *Shannon? Shannon O'Malley? Didn't she live in ...* "Ireland? Dad, you're sending me to Ireland to stay with Aunt Shannon? Are you crazy? You're pulling me out of school right at the end of the year, and sending me to stay with someone I don't even know for the whole summer? In *Ireland?*"

Her father looked up, his eyes moist. "I know that your aunt and I have had our differences over the years, but she's a fine woman. She'll take good care of you. I've already called her, and she agreed to have you stay for as long as I need to get things under control here." Kate O'Malley's sobs intensified. He looked over at her, and lowered his head into his hands again.

Molly collapsed into her chair and crossed her arms in exhaustion. *Oh boy,* she thought, *is this going to be a long summer.*

chapter two

The Emerald Isle

Chicago's O'Hare International Airport will intimidate all but the bravest of souls. It is one of the largest and busiest airports in the world. Molly certainly did not feel brave as she hurried along in the wake of her father's long strides down the terminal corridor.

Her small traveler suitcase bounced behind her, threatening to roll over every ten feet. She had to admire the way that her father handled her larger carry-on as it rolled smoothly across the tile. Of course, he had more experience rolling luggage through airports. Way too much experience.

"Dad," she gasped, "my arm is about to fall off. How much farther is the gate?"

Sean O'Malley glanced back at the small red-haired girl puffing behind him and slowed to a halt. "We still have a few minutes before boarding. Do you need to rest for a bit? We're already through the security checkpoint, so it's not going to take much time from here. We only have about five more gates."

Molly rested her suitcase on its legs and shook her arm like a wet noodle, which is about what it felt like. "Maybe if we just slowed down to a trot," she groused.

For the first time in two days, Mr. O'Malley seemed to genuinely smile. "Let's sit down over here for a bit. We have time. I keep forgetting you're just eleven, you've grown so much."

Molly sighed as she parked her case next to a vinyl seat on the end and plopped into it, swinging her feet with satisfaction. "Maybe if you'd check in on us more often, you'd notice things like that. Mom is worried. I hear her sometimes, talking to herself when she thinks I'm not listening, that I shouldn't be growing up so fast." She turned her intense green eyes to her father. "I don't feel like I can talk to the other kids about it. One, it's not their business. Two, I don't really have any close friends, because I try to help Mom out as much as I can."

Mr. O'Malley lowered himself into the seat next to her, pulling the other suitcase close to his knees. "Molly, we've been through all of this. That's why I came home. Your mom needs rest, and I need to have time with her right now. You know, you're a real trooper to go over and stay with Aunt Shannon. I really appreciate it."

"Like I had any choice in it," Molly said softly, looking down at her swinging feet. "It's just taking me away from you again, and it's taking me away from Mom, too! And even though I don't want you to go away again, *you're* the one that should be going to see Aunt Shannon! What is it between you two, anyway?"

Mr. O'Malley's smile faded as he sat back in the seat. "My big sister is disappointed in me." He leaned back further, lacing his fingers behind his head. "When I was twenty, I had the chance to get into a great job and get out of Ireland. I was able to travel all over the world, see new things

— in fact I met your mom on a business trip to Chicago. After we got married, we decided to live here. It's got a great airport" — he looked around the terminal — "yeah, a great airport."

"I don't understand. Why would getting a great job be disappointing to Aunt Shannon?"

"I never went back to Ireland. You have to understand, I came from a rural area, a very small village. Most people in Chicago work in a *building* that has more people in it than my entire home town does." He sighed and rubbed his eyes. "Your Aunt Shannon thinks I've abandoned my Irish roots. She's very traditional, very proud of Ireland and its history, and she feels like I betrayed that when I moved away."

"Why didn't you go back, Dad? I don't know much about Ireland, other than the St. Patrick's Day parade here in Chicago. You never took us to it or anything, but there was a lot on television. You go everywhere else in the world."

Mr. O'Malley shook his head slowly. "I couldn't wait to move away. I couldn't wait to get out of Murroogh."

"Mur-ook?" Molly repeated.

"That's how it's pronounced. It's spelled M-U-R-R-O-O-G-H, but sounding like a "k" on the end. There are less than a thousand people who live there, compared to over nine million in the Chicago area. But that's where I grew up."

"Does Aunt Shannon still live in Murroogh, then?"

"She does. I think she runs a bed and breakfast there, and something else, too ... I can't remember what at the moment. We haven't talked in a while. Until a couple of days ago."

Molly nodded and got to her feet. "I think I'm ready to go again." She grasped her suitcase handle and hobbled toward the steady stream of people walking to their gates. Turning, she asked, "Everything is okay for me to go over there?"

Mr. O'Malley stretched and rose to join her. "I'm sure everything is fine. You have your boarding pass. I'm sure glad your mother got you a passport when you two went up to Niagara Falls last year, even though you didn't technically need it then. That saves a lot of hassle, not to mention time, because you definitely need it to travel to Ireland. We're applying for a visa in case you need to stay longer than ninety days, and the airline is all set to give you every possible help as an unaccompanied minor... "

"Dad!" Molly interrupted in exasperation. "I mean, is it okay for me to stay with Aunt Shannon? Seeing how she feels about you— and maybe how she feels about me?"

Sean O'Malley stopped in surprise and looked at his daughter. "Oh ... oh, honey, don't worry about that. Your aunt and I may have differences, but she won't hold that against you! In fact, I think she is looking forward to having you there. She's never seen you, although I think your mom may have sent her some pictures."

"You think? You don't know?"

"No, Molly, I don't know." Mr. O'Malley grimaced. "I left it up to your mom to handle all of the correspondence and writing while I was out... "

"On business trips, I know." Molly finished for him.

They walked on together, stepping aside for the occasional service vehicle whining past. Finally gate M-21 appeared in the distance. *All the way at the end,* Molly moaned silently. The O'Malleys stepped into the long line at the gate counter to make sure that everything was in place for Molly's trip.

An older couple standing in front of them was arguing loudly. "I told you that suitcase was too heavy," the man rasped. His traveling companion, probably his wife, thought Molly, glared back at him. "So it was too heavy! It's just a little extra charge to get it on the plane. Would you rather carry two suitcases?"

The man shook his head in disgust. "What d'ya need all of that stuff for? We're only going for two weeks! We won't be able to get all of the bags in the car as it is!"

The couple continued their bickering as Molly turned to her father. "Are they going to Ireland, too?" she whispered. "Yes," he whispered back. "This is a direct flight— next stop, Shannon Airport."

Molly's eyes opened wide. "They named the airport after Aunt Shannon?"

"What — oh, no, honey, that's just a coincidence. Shannon is a popular name in Ireland. Shannon Airport is a major airport in Ireland, and it's the closest to where you are going."

"What is a co-ins-a-dents?"

"It just means that there is no real relationship between the two things, that one of the things didn't cause the other thing. For example, the fact that these people in front of us are flying on the same plane with you today is a coincidence. They didn't decide to go to Ireland because you are going there, and you aren't going to Ireland because of anything that they decided."

Molly scowled. "No, I'm going to Ireland because of something that *you* decided."

Mr. O'Malley looked down sadly at his daughter. "You're right, Molly. I'm afraid that is definitely *not* a coincidence." He laid a hand gently on her shoulder. "It will be all right, Molly."

She shrugged and turned to look at the line in front of her. The bickering couple was at the counter. They were now united against the gate agent while deciding where they would sit on the plane, their discussion of the luggage forgotten for the moment.

Her thoughts were interrupted by an unladylike growl from her stomach. Molly turned to her father with a grimace. "Dad, I'm getting hungry. I usually have dinner by this time."

"Hang on for a little bit. They'll serve dinner on the plane. If we had tried to get you something to eat earlier, you wouldn't have been hungry then. I thought the apple you had at home before we left would have taken care of you."

"Well, the apple helped. Maybe I worked up an appetite lugging this suitcase for three miles."

Mr. O'Malley laughed quietly. "I expect that's it."

"May I help you?" inquired the gate agent.

"Yes, thank you," replied Mr. O'Malley, stepping forward and handing her the ticket he was carrying. "My daughter is flying today as an unaccompanied minor. I want to make sure everything is in order for her."

The agent checked the information and smiled at the red-haired girl. "And you are Molly?" Molly nodded. "Welcome to American Airlines. We'll do everything we can so you will have a pleasant flight. Is this your first trip to Ireland?"

Molly nodded again. "I'm going to see my aunt."

"I see that we're traveling first class tonight. You have two carry-ons? Did you want to check either of these?"

"We're already at the checked baggage limit. I'm staying forever," Molly grumbled.

"We'll have someone help you with your bags, then, how will that be?" She tapped several keys on the console in front of her. "Did you want a window or aisle seat?"

"Window," Molly replied. "Why would anyone want an aisle seat in an airplane?"

"You'll understand when your legs get longer," Mr. O'Malley chimed in with a twinkle in his eye." The gate agent smiled as well. "All right, Molly, we have you in seat 4A straight through to Shannon. Enjoy your flight!" She inserted some papers into a slim document folder and handed it to Mr. O'Malley. "Just hand these to the attendant when we're ready to board. We'll be boarding first class in just a few minutes."

"Thank you," Mr. O'Malley smiled. "Grab your suitcase, Molly, time to sit for a little while longer."

Molly wearily rolled her suitcase back to the waiting area and slouched into a seat. Mr. O'Malley found a seat across from hers. Several announcements were made over the public address system for other flights and gates. Molly watched curiously as the lines formed to board at a nearby gate. Following her gaze, Mr. O'Malley yawned, "At least we won't have to go through that."

"Why not?" Molly asked.

"Because you're flying first class. They always board the first class passengers first. You'll be on the plane and enjoying a glass of ginger ale before the rest of the passengers start to board."

"That doesn't sound fair."

Mr. O'Malley squinted disapprovingly. "It's very fair. Your ticket for first class cost several times what economy class tickets go for."

"I thought you used your frequent flyer miles to get my ticket."

A smile creased Sean O'Malley's face. "Nothing gets by you, does it? You're right, I did use my miles to get your ticket. But I had to fly a lot of miles to earn them, let me tell you."

Molly sighed. "I know you did. I was sitting at home with Mom while you were earning them, remember?"

The loudspeaker came to life again. "Ladies and gentlemen, we are now boarding flight 256 to Shannon, Ireland. At this time we are boarding first class and passengers with small children only."

Looking relieved at the interruption, Mr. O'Malley said "That's you, honey," and rose to his feet. Molly dragged herself from the seat and followed him to the gate where a nice-looking young woman in a flight attendant's uniform greeted them.

"Good evening!" she said with a bright smile. "My name is Sheila. I understand we have a young person flying by herself today!"

"Yes, this is my daughter, Molly. She'll be meeting my sister, Shannon O'Malley at Shannon airport."

"Oh, they named the airport after your sister, then?" Sheila grinned.

"Told you," whispered Molly.

Mr. O'Malley smiled uneasily and managed, "Well, she's very modest."

"Don't worry about a thing. We'll make sure that Molly gets to her Aunt Shannon safe and sound. If I can just get your boarding pass... "

She took the card Mr. O'Malley offered and slid it under a scanner. "Seat 4A," she read as she returned the card. "I can help you with that extra carry-on. Are we ready to board?"

Molly nodded and looked up at her father. Her eyes brimmed with tears. "Take care of Mom."

"I will, sweetie. You take care of yourself. Don't be too much of a bother to your aunt."

"I won't, Dad. I'm only a bother to you." Molly turned and walked down the ramp, her suitcase bumping over the threshold, leaving a very uncomfortable looking Sean O'Malley standing at the gate. Sheila cleared her throat. "I— ah— guess I should get that carry-on now, Mr. O'Malley and catch up with her? Thank you, she'll be just fine!" She grabbed the handle and hurried after the departing girl.

"She'll be just fine," repeated Mr. O'Malley to himself. "What about the rest of us?"

———————

Why does it take so long to get going after all of the passengers are on? Molly thought to herself. She took another sip of her ginger ale. *At least Dad was right about something, this ginger ale is pretty good.*

"How are you doing, Molly?" Sheila paused by her seat, a miniature pillow in her hand. Sheila had been very kind, helping Molly put her luggage into the overhead bin and getting her settled in her seat.

"Fine, Sheila. Thank you." Molly glanced up at the flight attendant gratefully. "I feel guilty getting all this attention, though."

Sheila responded with a smile that made the sun come up. "Don't you worry about that! You deserve all the attention you can get. I'm really impressed that you are flying across the ocean all by yourself!"

Molly looked out the window where the ramp workers were still loading luggage into the belly of the plane from their electric trams. "I didn't have much choice. Mom's in the hospital, and Dad's too busy, like always." She sighed, and turned back to look at Sheila. "It's like I'm in the way, and Dad wants to ship me off to Ireland so he can" — she crooked her index and middle fingers on each hand to indicate quotes— *"deal* with things."

"Yeah," Sheila exhaled. "I think I caught some of that. Since we can't change any of that now, maybe we could leave that back at the gate and concentrate on getting you safely to your Aunt Shannon. The flight takes just a little over seven hours. We will be serving your dinner on the plane as soon as we are in the air, and you don't want to miss my cooking!" She winked mischievously. "I recommend that you try to get some sleep after that, because it will be early morning there when we land. I brought you a pillow for your head, and we can recline your seat a little bit after you're through with your dinner. Is there anything else I can do for you?"

"Yes," said Molly while picking up a pretzel. "Can you adjust the air conditioner vent for me? I can't reach the controls while I'm sitting down." She extended her other arm to demonstrate.

"Certainly," Sheila replied. "Do you want it colder, warmer, or off?"

"Colder. It's a little warm in here."

Sheila nodded as she set the vent controls. "It's often a little warm until we switch over to the plane's internal power. As soon as we back away from the gate it will get cooler." She snapped to attention and delivered a mock salute. "Flight attendant Sheila Carter requesting permission to attend to other passengers!"

Molly grinned and returned the salute. "Dismissed!"

Things were a little scary for Molly when the plane took off. She was sure that they were going to crash at the end of the runway, they were moving fast, faster than she had ever gone in a car. Then the bumping stopped as the plane lifted into the air, and only the solid thumps of the landing gear retracting reminded her that they had ever been on wheels at all.

The dinner wasn't bad, but Molly had to remind herself that she was in first class, after all. Sheila was as good as her word, helping Molly adjust her seat back and making sure she was comfortable. At least as comfortable as one can get in a seat that only tilts back a couple of inches.

Darkness came swiftly outside the small windows of the airplane as they fled from the sun. The steady throb of the jet engines worked its magic on Molly as her eyes closed. Sheila came by and stretched a light blanket over her. Molly sleepily pulled the blanket up to her lightly freckled chin without waking.

"Well," Sheila whispered, "I hope that things work out as peacefully for you as you look now." She tiptoed away.

"Thank you," whispered Molly in her sleep.

———————

Molly couldn't decide what woke her— whether it was a change in the rhythm of the engines, a gradual slowing of the airplane's speed or the weak light of the dawn peeking through the side window. She shifted in her seat to look outside, but could see only white clouds.

"Good morning!" Sheila greeted her merrily. Molly looked at her and rubbed her eyes. "Do you ever sleep?" she mumbled.

"Only when I'm not on duty. Would you like a pastry and some juice?"

Molly nodded and moved the pillow to the seat beside her. "Where are we? It seems like I just fell asleep."

"We're getting close now, probably another fifteen minutes or so before you can see anything— and that's if the weather is clear. I'll get your breakfast."

The girl rummaged through her purse for a comb. Finding it, she pulled it carefully through her shock of red hair. It was always unmanageable in the morning. Molly thought it was a darn shame that she had her brush packed away. Looking at her dim reflection in the tiny window, she nodded in satisfaction. It would have to do until she could get to a real mirror.

The sugar rush from her pastry helped revive her, so Molly was almost awake when the plane slowed again and slid down into the clouds. Molly watched disinterestedly as the featureless vapor outside closed in. Then she gasped.

As they dropped out of the clouds, a wide expanse of blue ocean unfolded to kiss the shores of a lush green coastline. Even from this distance, Molly could make out hills dotting the landscape, sweeping up from the water.

Sheila leaned over her shoulder. "They don't call it the Emerald Isle for nothing, do they?" she sighed. "I love it every time I see it."

"Why do they call it the Emerald Isle? Are there lots of emeralds there?" Molly inquired.

"Mmmm ... no, I don't think so. It's called the Emerald Isle because of the color. Everything is green all the time, like an emerald."

Molly was surprised. "It's green in the winter, too? But I looked on a globe, and Ireland is way north of where Chicago is. We get lots of snow and everything in the winter."

"As I understand it, there is a flow of warm water from the Gulf of Mexico that runs across the Atlantic Ocean. It's called the Gulf Stream. That helps keep the water around Ireland warm, and the prevailing winds are from the southwest, where it's warmer. Both of those things help Ireland maintain a moderate climate."

Molly frowned as she thought. "And moderate means not hot, and not cold either?"

Sheila nodded as she expertly began packing blankets and pillows into the overhead bins. "It's good to keep a jacket handy— it can get pretty cool in Ireland, but it hardly ever freezes. And it can rain at any minute. It rarely gets up to ninety degrees Fahrenheit. It gets hotter when it's hot and colder when it's cold as you travel inland, away from the sea."

The flight attendant checked Molly's seat belt and made sure her seat was not reclined. "Keep a look out the window. You see where it looks like a huge lake there? That's actually the Shannon River, and it's the longest river in

Ireland. It's ten miles across at its mouth and bulges to six and seven miles wide in places upstream. We're going to fly up it for a ways. Shannon Airport is right on the bank." She gave Molly one last smile. "You've been great on this flight, Molly! I have to check the other passengers again and prepare for landing. I'll be back after we land."

"Thank you, Sheila! I'll look for the river." Molly looked out her window as Sheila hurried off.

What first looked like a vast bay between two far-flung peninsulas began to narrow slightly. *So that's the Shannon River,* Molly thought. *Do they have to name everything in Ireland after Aunt Shannon?* If Sheila hadn't told her it was a river, she would have thought it to be a long arm of the sea that had pounded its way into the island. She could tell that it was really, really wide.

Up ahead she could see the river widen again, with a huge arm fanning off to her left. As the plane passed by the area she saw an airport below, perched on the banks of the river. *We're going to miss it,* she thought in alarm. Then the plane started to bank to the left, making a long, lazy circle in the sky. *Okay, we're coming back to it,* she comforted herself, hoping that no one noticed her anguish. *Stop acting like a kid.*

For a few minutes the plane seemed to hang suspended in the sky. The trees and houses started getting bigger and bigger — and then they started to go by faster and faster. It didn't seem quite as fast as when they took off. The landing gear unfolded with a whine and a jerk, slowing them down even more.

They flew over a road and the ground opened up into a field. Suddenly the runway was below them, and the plane floated like a beach ball that fights being forced under water. There was a slight bump as the wheels touched the asphalt and the rubber screeched in protest. Molly gripped the arms of her seat as the plane braked heavily.

Then it was over. The plane taxied quietly along the runway as if it had been an uneventful flight. Which it was, except to the small red-haired girl in seat 4A.

Sheila's voice came over the intercom. "Ladies and gentlemen, welcome to Shannon International Airport and the Republic of Ireland."

"Well," Molly breathed, "I'm here."

chapter three

Shannon O'Malley

One of the grand things about flying first class is that you don't have to wait for all of the people ahead of you to get off of the plane first. Instead, all of the people behind you have to wait for *you* to get off the plane.

For Molly, it was a mixed blessing. Sheila helped her get all of her luggage together, but Molly dreaded what she would find at the end of the ramp. The cold aluminum aircraft offered more comfort than an aunt she had never seen, and a country she knew nothing about.

"Molly," said Sheila, "we have another agent who will take you through customs. Your aunt should be waiting right inside the terminal. It's been wonderful having you with us, and I really hope you'll have a nice stay."

Molly nodded and squeezed her hand. A young man in a gate agent's uniform smiled at Molly and led her down the hallway, rolling her larger carry-on behind him. Everything was pretty much a blur for Molly as she went through customs, and the agent led her through a final doorway. A woman's voice said "Molly?"

She turned to see an attractive woman with dark auburn hair whose appearance matched the few pictures she had seen at home. The woman wore khaki slacks, with a light jacket draped over her pink blouse.

"Aunt Shannon?"

Shannon O'Malley enveloped the girl in a tight embrace, then stood back to look at her. "My, how you've grown! I think my last pictures of ya are at least a year old!" Turning to the gate agent, she said "Thank ya for your help! I think we can manage from here."

She took the large carryon from the agent in one hand, and Molly's hand in the other. "Let's go find a cart for the rest of your luggage, shall we? I don't think we have enough hands between the two of us."

Molly nodded mutely. *I think I like her already. But that doesn't make it right that I was sent here.*

Soon the sizeable pile of luggage delivered to the baggage carousel was stacked on a rolling cart that Shannon enlisted. "Is that all of it, then, Molly?"

"Isn't it enough?" Molly grumbled in return.

Shannon paused to regard her niece. "I'll thank ya not to be takin' that tone with *me*, young lady. We've both been put in a bit of a situation here. We'll talk about this in the car. Do I make myself clear, now?"

"Yes, ma'am." Molly bit her lip.

The car was very small. There was plenty of room for Molly and her aunt in the front, but the luggage barely fit into the back even with the rear seat folded down. Molly stared in amazement at the front seat. "The steering wheel is on the right side of the car!"

Shannon smiled as she slid into the seat behind the steering wheel. "That's because we drive on the left side of the road over here."

"Doesn't that cause a lot of accidents?"

"Not really. We allow only the bravest American tourists to drive a car by themselves. Now hop in on the other side and buckle up. I'll be driving today."

It started to rain as they drove away from the airport. "Now Molly, dear, I gather from your comment at the baggage area that you're not keen on being here. I want ya to know that it's not coming at the best time for me, either." Shannon looked carefully to her right as she turned left onto the highway. "When your father called, it was a complete surprise. You're family, and I'm very happy to see ya. But I want ya to know that things are going to be a little tough for a few weeks."

"What do you mean, tough?"

"Well, it's not the way I want things to be. I work two jobs, Molly. In the mornings I help Mrs. Walsh at her bed and breakfast. When that's done I drive down to Doolin to work at O'Conner's pub until late. It's a miracle I was able to get the time off to pick ya up at all today. The problem is that I won't be able to spend any time with ya for at least a couple of weeks. I don't feel proper leaving ya at the house by yourself, but I've no choice."

Molly nodded. "I understand about not having a choice, Aunt Shannon."

The rain made it difficult to see. Shannon peered through the windshield. "It's a good thing I know the roads here. This downpour is not making things easy. Now the weather report says we'll have rain for the next week."

"Does it always rain in Ireland?"

"It rains quite a bit, dear. I live on the coast, so the weather tends to change more quickly. It can rain in the morning, the sun will come out by lunch, and another storm will come in by the afternoon. But we have our fine days, too. Don't ya have bad days in Chicago?"

"Mostly in the winter, when we have snow."

"We don't get much snow here. I can't really remember when we had snow last, it's been a couple of years, anyway, and then only for a day."

They traveled through a couple of good sized towns, and then through lush green countryside. The road looked awfully narrow to Molly. Walls covered in green bushes lay just inches from the pavement. In spots, she thought she saw jagged rocks poking out between the leaves. "Aunt Shannon, are those rocks in the walls by the road?"

"The walls are all made of rocks. The hazel grows over it, but most of the roads in Ireland have rock walls on both sides. Ya get used to it, but most visitors find it amazing that we have so many miles of rock wall built up. There are plenty of rocks to build with here, that's for certain."

Molly was quiet for the rest of the trip. Another hour passed before they turned off the main road and climbed up a short driveway. Molly looked through the rain that was still falling at a modest cream-colored house. "Here's home for a while, dear," Shannon announced. "Let's get your things inside and I'll fix us some lunch."

They rolled the suitcases through the front door. "I've got your bedroom over here. I think it will be just fine for ya. Before ya unpack, do ya want something to eat?"

"Sure."

The kitchen was in the back of the house. Molly looked out the window to see a tall, rocky hill that towered over the landscape. "What is that?"

"That would be the Burren, if you mean the hill— or the start of the Burren, anyway. It's the edge that comes up to the coast. Did ya check out the front window?"

Molly walked back to the living room and peeked through the window. Beyond a couple of hundred yards of pasture and a few more houses was a large body of water. After that, the mist obscured everything. "Is that a lake or something?" Molly asked.

"That's Galway Bay. You're looking out into the Atlantic Ocean in that direction. Ya can't see them now for the rain, but over to your left are the Aran Islands. Maybe we can take the ferry over if we get a nice day."

"So we're in between the ocean and a mountain?"

"Ya could put it that way," Shannon smiled, "Although it's not so much a mountain as it is a tall hill. I can probably take ya up some time."

"That's all right," Molly replied. "I think I'm ready for something to eat."

Shannon made two ham and cheese sandwiches on slices of thick brown bread slathered with mayonnaise, and poured them two cups of hot tea. "What is this?" Molly asked, pointing to the steaming liquid.

"Just hot tea. It'll warm ya up nicely. Have you ever tried it with milk?" Molly shook her head. "Give it a go," Shannon encouraged her. "Ya might like it. There's brown sugar on the table, too, scoop a couple of spoons of that into it to sweeten it up."

Cautiously Molly poured a little bit of milk into the brown tea, turning it a creamy shade of tan. After mixing the sugar in, she found it quite satisfactory.

In the afternoon Molly took a nap. When she woke refreshed, she found Aunt Shannon busy straightening up the house. "Not much time to do cleaning, with two jobs," she apologized. "Now let's talk about what ya need to be doing for the next couple of weeks. Your dad said that ya brought school books with ya?"

"Yes. All of the assignments from the last two weeks of the term."

"Well, that's a good thing. Ya can work on your school work while I go to my jobs during the day. I'm sure that won't be much fun, but it will give ya something to do."

Molly nodded glumly.

"It's all right, dear," said Shannon. "Things will get better over time."

"Aunt Shannon?"

"Yes, Molly?"

"Are you mad at me?"

Shannon sat down on a kitchen chair. "Come here, dear." Molly walked hesitantly to her Aunt, who drew her up close with a hug. "I'm not a bit mad at ya for coming to see me. It's the first time I've seen my niece, and I am delighted. Nevertheless, I won't have ya speak disrespectfully to me or to anyone else. If ya have a problem, talk plainly about it. Ya don't have to be sarcastic with me, especially when ya don't even know me well yet."

"Are you mad at my dad, then?"

Shannon looked away for a second. "Whew! So that's it. Yes, I *do* have a few bones to pick with your dad, but that has nothing to do with you! I'll not project any problems I have with your father onto ya, that wouldn't be fair at all. Now that we're talking plainly, though, do ya have some problems with your dad yourself?"

Molly looked at her aunt closely. "Talking plainly, did you just change the subject?" she asked, followed closely by a wink.

Shannon's face was expressionless. Molly wondered *did I go too far*? Then Shannon erupted in laughter. "My, ya are adorable!" and hugged her closer.

Tears were streaming down her face by the time she released Molly. "Come pull up a chair, dear. We girls need to have a talk."

Over cups of steaming hot chocolate, Molly confided her fears about her family falling apart, and being away from them during this difficult time. Shannon talked freely on her part about her brother.

"Sean didn't think he fit in here in Ireland. Perhaps back then, he didn't. Ireland has changed since he left to make his fortune in the world. We're much more modern here than we used to be. Maybe I'm the one who's out of place now." She brushed her dark hair behind her ear. "Ireland used to be a place of magic, full of stories and traditional music every night. Maybe that's why I keep my job at the pub in Doolin."

"They have music there?"

"Oh, yes." Shannon's eyes seemed to be looking far away. "Every night at about half-nine nearly every pub in Doolin has traditional Irish music."

"Half nine?"

Shannon refocused her eyes on Molly. "That's how we say nine-thirty here. You'll get used to it, dear."

"And Dad doesn't like Irish music?"

"I don't think he likes Irish anything. Has he ever taught ya anything about Ireland?"

"No. We talked about it a little at the airport. He thinks you are mad at him for 'abandoning his Irish roots,' whatever that means."

Shannon nodded. "He could be right. I think ya can keep your heritage at the same time ya make your way in the world. I love the history of Ireland, the wonderful things we have here." She sighed. "I really pity Sean. He has missed out on so much."

Molly looked down at her feet. She didn't really want to take her father's side on this. At the same time she felt badly to hear her aunt talk about her dad that way.

"There's so much that has been lost here in Ireland. There aren't as many people in Ireland now as there were long ago, and the ones that are left don't remember or don't share the stories like they used to." Shannon yawned and stretched. "That's probably enough for tonight. I don't know about you, girl, but this old lady has about had it."

"You're not old, Aunt Shannon!"

"Well, thank ya, Molly. I think both of us need to be getting to bed right now. We'll get up very early tomorrow and I'll fix ya an Irish breakfast before I leave."

Molly's room was small but functional. It was across the hall from her aunt's bedroom, and her window looked out on the Burren hill.

She felt refreshed after her afternoon nap, but she could tell that something was different, as if she was going to be tired again. "This is probably that jet lag that Dad talks about," she yawned. "I may as well unpack what I can tonight before I fall asleep again."

A chest of drawers held her clothes nicely. She pulled her hairbrush through her slightly bushy red hair and admired the result in the mirror that hung on the bathroom door with satisfaction. She laid the brush on top of the chest of drawers, deciding her things for the bathroom could wait until morning.

The final suitcase held her books from school. She piled them unceremoniously on the small table by the door. "The airline just couldn't lose *that* suitcase, could they?" Molly scowled.

She pulled on her pajamas and tossed her clothes into the hamper Aunt Shannon had provided. Turning on the small lamp on the nightstand, she slipped under the sheets, plumping her pillow behind her back. She pulled up the heart shaped locket that hung from a silver chain around her neck and stared quietly at it before opening it up.

Each half of the locket held a picture of one of Molly's parents. Her dad was in the left side, his sure, confident smile radiating out from the photograph. Her mom sat quietly on the right side, her eyes sparkling with a happiness that Molly had not seen for a long time.

"We *were* happy once. We'll work everything out, I just *know* it!" She slowly closed the locket and laid it carefully on the nightstand. Switching the lamp off, she laid her head on the pillow, which was somehow damp right by her eye, and waited for sleep to come.

The next morning Molly woke up to delicious smells coming from the kitchen. A place was set for her at the table, with a small pitcher of milk and a pot of hot tea. Brown bread and jam filled small wicker baskets, and a glass of orange juice was already poured.

"Good morning, sleepyhead!" her aunt greeted her. "You're just in time." She set a plate filled with scrambled eggs and some things Molly didn't recognize in front of the girl. "I don't know that you'll like all of this, but we'll find out what ya do like, and ya can leave the rest."

Molly knew she could never eat everything on that plate, but she was determined to try some of everything. There were sausage links that tasted less meaty than what they had back in Chicago, but were still pretty good. The scrambled eggs were familiar, and she could tell that Aunt Shannon knew how to whip them up just right. The potatoes had been diced and cooked in butter, making her mouth water. The "bacon" looked more like a thin slice of ham, but had a little bit of the bacon flavor that she remembered from back home.

Other mysteries remained. Two small round patties of what looked like meat lay on the plate. The larger one was a light tan color, with flecks of color running through it. The smaller was much darker, almost black. Molly tried tiny bites of each. The lighter colored one was okay, tasting a little mealy, but the dark one was too bitter for Molly's taste. "What are these, Aunt Shannon?"

"That's white and black pudding. The white is meat and fillings, with oatmeal and other things. The black is meat and filler cooked with blood, which makes it so dark. Ya don't like the black, then?"

Molly shook her head. "That's all right, dear, I'll know not to fix the black pudding for ya next time. Now ya can shock your friends when ya tell them what your aunt fed ya over here!"

Molly grinned and took a drink of her orange juice. "I'm stuffed. This brown bread and tea with milk in it is sooo good."

"I'm glad ya like it! Now I've got to run off to work. We can't really have breakfast like this every day, so I'll leave ya something ya can fix yourself. There's cereal, I think ya can handle the teapot, and here's the microwave if ya want to heat something up on a plate."

"What about lunch?" Molly asked.

"Check the refrigerator, there should be stuff in there to make a sandwich or two. The brown bread ya like so much is over here on the counter. Ya can heat up a frozen dinner tonight." She untied her apron and hung it up on a peg. "I'm off to the Walsh's, then. I'll see ya tonight, dear." She gave Molly a quick kiss on the forehead.

As she opened the door, she let out a groan. "Still raining, and no sign of it stopping!" Molly watched as she ran for the car and drove down the driveway onto the main road.

It continued to rain that day and the next. Molly spent time working on her assignments. It was harder in some ways, not having a teacher to explain things to you. There were advantages, too, as Molly could spend more time reading in her science book. The pictures were wonderful, and she read about orchids that lived in the tropical rain forest. Also interesting were the flowers of the arctic and the tundra that Mr. Henderson had talked about her last day in school. The *Dryas octopetala* was an easy one to remember. 'Octo' is obviously eight, like an octopus, and 'petala' is just petals. A *Dryas octopetala* flower has eight petals.

Other than her school work, the days stretched into endless boredom. The sun came up at five in the morning, and sunset waited until ten at night. Aunt Shannon explained to Molly that since Ireland was so far north, the sun stayed up much longer during the summer, making the days almost 18 hours long.

That is, when you could see the sun. It rained nearly every day, cloaking the coastline with gray reflected from the clouds above. It was positively dreary, like Kansas in the Wizard of Oz, where everything was gray and there was no color at all.

The view of the Burren was even worse. The nearby hill was impressive, towering above the village that clung to the shoreline, but it was covered almost completely with rocks with only thin strips of gray-green to hint that any life was there.

One morning Shannon had a few minutes before she had to leave for the day. Molly took the opportunity to ask, "Is it pretty from up on top of the hill, Aunt Shannon?"

"It is when the sun is out. The walk up is beautiful, too. Just over the stone wall there is the green road, that's mostly grass until ya get to the wall that goes to the top. Then it's mostly rock."

Science and Math, English and Social Studies all kept Molly busy for the first week and a half. It wasn't as if she had missed the whole year, though. The chapters ran out all too quickly, the papers and quizzes were filled out, and then there simply was nothing left for an eleven year old girl to do.

Gradually Molly formed a plan to escape the boredom. And she didn't tell anyone.

chapter four

Escape

On a cool Thursday morning, Aunt Shannon left for her job at the bed and breakfast. Molly waited until she heard the car drive well down the road. She pulled on her jeans, laced up her sneakers and pulled a sweatshirt over her head.

The refrigerator yielded all of the bounty needed for a good lunch — mayonnaise, pickles, slices of cheese (not American) and some sausage leftover from breakfast. Brown bread sliced medium thick soon wrapped Molly's creation, which she packaged up into a bag. She threw in some potato chips (that Aunt Shannon insisted on calling crisps) and an apple for good measure. She emptied her backpack of books, stacking them precariously on the desk's edge, then loaded her lunch and added two bottles of water.

"I've never done anything like this before," Molly muttered as she shouldered her backpack. "But then, I've never been abandoned in such a desolate place before!" She looked out to the ocean, where for a change the sun sparkled off the water. Today she could see the three Aran Islands easily, lined up across the bay in the hazy distance.

Today was not the day for water and the coastline, however. Climbing over the stone wall, she saw a wide stretch of grassy pasture running along the hillside. "The green road," she murmured. The view across Galway Bay was as beautiful as her aunt had promised, with the Aran Islands becoming clearer to the west, and the Galway coastline clearly visible to the north. After walking for about a half hour, she turned her face to the early sun that was casting shadows across the broken landscape of the Burren. Carefully she picked her way across the irregular limestone. It wouldn't do to turn an ankle here, all by herself.

The hills behind Murroogh were surprisingly steep, rising quickly from the sleepy coastal village. Molly aimed for a low ridge that would take her over the hills to what she assumed would be more rocks beyond. After laboring for the better part of an hour, she reached the ridge and continued on a plateau.

It looked like a moonscape, with rocks jutting up from the ground everywhere. Yet in the cracks between the rocks, Molly noticed green plants that had taken hold. Every once in a while she spotted a flash of color.

"An *orchid*? Here? My science book said that orchids grew in the tropics!" She bent to examine the flower more closely. It sure looked like the picture in the book.

She moved on, looking now for more flowers. When she looked up to give her eyes a rest, she saw something that seemed to be out of place. Curious, she walked toward it.

At first it appeared to be rocks piled up to make a low wall. As Molly drew closer she could tell that it was definitely man-made. The stones had been arranged in a nearly perfect circle, the walls up to ten feet high. One section had pretty much fallen down, allowing her to scramble over the rubble.

"What is this?" Molly asked herself. She decided to sit down on a flat rock and have her lunch. She spread her sandwich and crisps out on a napkin, and munched contentedly while thinking about her find.

Molly washed her picnic down with half a bottle of water and packed up the rest, planning to save her apple for a snack later. "Perhaps I'll just go a little further that way, and then go back," she decided. She climbed out of the rock circle and started across the stark panorama.

The view from outside the rock circle was wonderful. Molly could see lots of water surrounding her on one side, and hills climbing still higher on the other.

Not far away, she saw some more green between the rocks. Stooping to investigate, she dropped to her knees in surprise. "I don't believe this! *Dryas octopetala* here? That grows in the tundra! But Ireland stays warm because of the Gulf Stream — at least that's what Sheila said!" She almost began to wish she had brought her science book along to compare the plants with the pictures, even though the book was heavy.

A sudden uneasiness came over her. Looking around for a possible cause, what she saw dismayed her. Where there had been bright sunshine only minutes before, there was now a thick fog that softened the sharp edges of the rock and blotted out the sun. Molly could not see the rock circle any more, and her unease increased to a near panic.

"I think it's this way!" she said, and headed off through the fog. Although she tried to be careful, the mist soon made the rocks slippery, and she scraped her ankles a couple of times on the sharp edges. The fog blanketed all sound except for Molly's raspy breathing.

On and on she went, stumbling over the slick stones, bruising her knee once. Her eyes stung from the tears, and she blinked again and again, hoping that she would see better in a moment. The fog seemed to grow thicker and more menacing instead.

An hour passed, and Molly knew that she had missed the rock pile in the murky fog. She was utterly, totally lost. She sat down on a large rock, exhausted, and began to sob. Her frame heaved with the emotions raging through her.

"Why did Dad have to spend so much time at work? Why did he leave it up to Mom to take care of us? Why did Mom have to get sick? Why did they dump me over here in this horrible place? Why did I come out here today? I'm so stupid!" She sniffed loudly. "I'm going to die!"

Molly buried her head in her arms and sobbed again. Finally her sobs grew quieter. She stopped and raised her tear-stained face.

"Do I hear something?" she whispered. She froze, hardly daring to breathe. She strained to hear what the sound was, if it was there at all.

Ahhh ... there it was again. Very faint, very soft, but very clearly a buzzing noise that was not made by the wind.

Molly couldn't see very far, but she could let the sound guide her. Carefully she minced her way through the angled rocks toward the buzz. *Careful— don't slip again, your ankles are throbbing enough already,* she thought.

Gradually a low rock shelf materialized in the fog. The sound seemed to be coming from the other side, below the top. Slowly Molly crawled onto the top of the slab and inched toward the edge. She lay flat and looked down where the noise was coming from.

Lying comfortably with his head cradled on a tiny knapsack was a man, snoring contentedly. He wore a brown leather apron. A half-made shoe lay beside him, apparently having slipped off of his lap during his slumber. His hair was black as midnight, and his own feet were clad in the most exquisite leather shoes, each adorned with a bright buckle. His clothes were rough but well-kept; his trousers a dark shade of green and his shirt a brick red. A small hammer lay on his chest, his hand still grasping the handle.

The most amazing thing about the man was that he was only two feet tall.

Molly gaped at the miniature man for what seemed like an eternity before deciding to talk to him. Tiny or not, maybe he could help her get back to Aunt Shannon's house. "Excuse me," she whispered. "I wonder if you could help me?"

The man's snoring ceased and he stirred slightly. Slowly he cracked one eye open. He lay there for another second, opened both eyes wide and leaped to his feet, his hammer thudding to the ground. "By the stars! Whoareyah, and what isit that ye be wantin'?"

Molly put on the best smile she could muster. "I'm Molly O'Malley, and I was wondering if you could help me find my way back to my Aunt Shannon's house in Murroogh."

The little man shook his head as though he couldn't believe what he was hearing. "Are ye daft, girl? Do ye not know who you're dealin' with here?"

"I'm not daft, I'm lost. And now that you mention it, I *don't* know who I'm dealing with. You haven't introduced yourself yet!" Molly folded her hands under her chin.

He stared at her in amazement. "You've plenty of cheek, I'll grant ye that!" Drawing himself up to his full height, he made a sweeping bow from the waist. "Paddy Finegan, at your service. Now if you'll excuse me, I must be gettin' on me way." He retrieved his shoe, and tucked the hammer into his belt.

"Oh, Mr. Finegan, please don't leave yet! I really am lost, and I need your help to get back home! I'm sorry that I surprised you, but I didn't know what else to do!" Molly's green eyes filled with tears again.

Paddy stopped and gave her a hard look. "Sure, and don't ye think that I have more wits about me than to trust a big 'un? I've dealt with your kind before. I know what it is that you're after!"

Molly blinked in frank astonishment. "I don't know what you mean. I just want some help so I can get home!" She sat up, her lip quivering. "I guess I'm just a bother to everyone around me!"

"Now, don't ye be trying to pull that 'sad little me' trick on old Paddy! It's been tried before! You'll not be hoodwinkin' this leprechaun so easily!"

Molly looked sadly at the wee man, as if she had just seen him for the first time. "Le-le-leprechaun?"

Paddy groaned in exasperation and threw the shoe to the ground. "You're good, I'll give ye that! Now don't be tellin' me that ye don't know what a leprechaun is!"

"But I don't. I've never been to Ireland before!"

Paddy began to pace, waving his hands in front of him. "Ye don't have to have been to Eire to know about leprechauns! We're famous around the world! What part of the world be ye from, girl?"

"Chicago," Molly said.

"That would be America, then? How could ye not be knowin' about leprechauns?"

Molly looked down in despair. "I don't know anything about Ireland. My dad never wanted to talk about where he came from."

Paddy wheeled to face the girl, his finger pointed at her in victory. "Aha! I know what it is! It's me gold you're after! Everyone knows that a leprechaun has a crock o' gold that he's scrimped and saved for all o' his hard life! You're tryin' to trick poor Paddy Finegan into givin' away his gold!"

Molly raised her face and looked square into Paddy's eyes. When she spoke, she almost spat the words out. "Gold?! Why in the world would I want your gold? Gold is all that my father cares about, making money, giving us money, never giving us any time or love. Gold." She crossed her arms and turned away. "Gold is what is tearing our family apart. Why would I want your gold?"

Paddy stood like a statue in the park, his arm stretched out to point at Molly. The smile drained from his face as he realized how silly he must look. Sheepishly he dropped his arm to his side, and looked up at the girl, who made no move to turn back to him. "Ahem. Ye know, th' usual approach is to never take your eyes off o' a leprechaun, or they'll go away."

"You said you were going to go away anyway. So go. Just leave me alone out here in the Burren to die. Go back to your gold and your friends."

Paddy sat down on a stone and picked up the shoe again. He sighed. "Either you're th' best con artist I've ever met in me brief life, or it's truly lost ye are. Never have I met anyone who didn't want me gold." He looked up again. "And I don't have that many friends."

Molly wiped a tear from her cheek and turned back to Paddy. "I am lost, Paddy. I'm lost in this dreadful fog, and I'm lost in this dreadful Burren in this dreadful country, and I should never have left Aunt Shannon's house to come out here. Why can't you believe that?"

Paddy tapped a stone with the toe of the unfinished shoe. "Aye, it can be a dreadful place." He lowered his voice and murmured quietly, "And dreadful things are happenin' all over…"

"Don't you care about anything except your stupid gold? Do you care about anything?" Molly blurted.

He looked up from his reverie with a wicked grin. "Now there's a switch for ye! A human begging a favor from a nasty leprechaun! The rest of 'em will like to hear ... " He broke off suddenly, placing his hand quickly over his lips.

"The rest of *who?*" Molly probed, leaning forward. "There's *more* of you? Are they close by?"

"Well, Paddy, here's another fine mess you've gotten yourself into," Paddy grumbled. "No, girl, I'll not be givin' away any news about me fellow leprechauns. You'll be seein' none o' their gold!"

Molly's mouth scrunched up into a pout. "I'm not interested in their gold, I was hoping they would be able help me get back home, since you apparently can't find your way off of the Burren."

"Can't find me way ... what is it that you're implyin' ... " Paddy sputtered. "It's a fine thing for *you* to talk about someone not bein' able to find their way off o' th' Burren, in this *dreadful fog* and all," he mimicked Molly's earlier plea.

Molly looked at the defiant leprechaun. He stood with his arms planted on his hips and a smirk smeared across his face. "You're not really very happy here, are you, Paddy? What's happened to make you so sad?"

Paddy's face contorted in surprise and denial. "Not — what are ye going on about, girl?" He clasped his hands behind his back and took a few nervous steps back and forth. "I have a grand life here! There's no beatin' th' weather in Eire, so long as ye don't mind th' rain, and there's not a lot o' intruders come to interrupt me while I'm workin' out here in th' Burren ... except the botanists and a tourist that gets lost once in a while."

"You keep saying 'Eire'... is that short for Ireland?"

Paddy sighed. "Eire *is* Ireland. It's th' old Irish tongue, the Gaelic language. Now don't ye be changin' the subject... "

"Well, you keep bringing up new things. All of this is new to me, and when I hear something new, I start to think about it. Like when you mentioned botanists just now. In our science class in school, we learned that botanists are scientists who study plants." Molly furrowed her brow in thought. "Like the orchid I saw earlier. How can an orchid survive this far north? They grow in between the rocks. They're beautiful. And I'm certain I saw a *Dryas octopetala*. That grows in the tundra."

Sitting down wearily on a stone, Paddy scratched his head. "I've never met anyone like you, that's for certain," he sighed. "Not interested in gold, taken with a wee flower growin' between th' rocks, wantin' to know why *I'm* sad." He looked up at the red haired girl, who was now looking at him expectantly. "What is it ye want from me?"

"Why don't you trust me, Paddy? Do I look like I'm a threat to you?" Molly's green eyes shone with the tears that were ready to start again at any moment.

"Centuries of history, girl. Ye come from a race o' big 'uns that have always looked for power and wealth. We leprechauns have had to use all o' our wits to stay alive."

"Well, I'm not looking for power and wealth. I only want to get back home. Why won't you help me?"

Paddy rubbed his chin thoughtfully. "There may be a way, Molly O'Malley."

Molly looked at him hopefully. "What do you mean?"

Paddy smiled, set his shoe down beside him, and rubbed his hands together. "Would ye be willin' to answer seven questions?"

chapter five

Seven Questions

Molly looked at the leprechaun in wonder. "Seven questions?" she repeated. "What kind of questions?"

"Th' kind o' questions that will reveal your true nature," Paddy replied with a grin. "There's no one can best a leprechaun in matchin' wits. I'll know whether I can trust ye after ye answer th' seven questions."

"All right, Paddy, on one condition." Molly sat up and dangled her feet over the rock ledge.

"Condition? Now who said anythin' about allowin' conditions?" Paddy snarled.

"Now don't start getting angry," Molly said sweetly, "but fair is fair. If you get to ask me seven questions, I get to ask *you* seven questions as well."

"Ask *me* seven questions? That's ridiculous! A big 'un askin' a leprechaun questions! It's never been done!" He folded his arms and planted his feet firmly apart. "I won't have it!"

"Aren't you trustworthy, Paddy? You have an honest face."

His jaw dropped as he stared at Molly. "Of course I'm trustworthy!" he protested as he crossed his fingers behind his back.

Molly smiled. "Well, then, there's no reason for you to be concerned about a stranger lost in the Burren asking you a few questions, too. You have nothing to hide. You're a trustworthy person."

The leprechaun sighed. "Very well, then. Let's go to a fittin' place for such a task as th' Seven Questions. Follow me."

Paddy skipped over the rocks, hopping from one to the next like a gazelle skipping across the plains. Molly threaded her backpack over her arms and followed carefully, determined not to fall again. "Paddy, slow down a bit, would you? These rocks are slippery!"

He stopped and looked at her with concern. "Have ye hurt yourself, then?"

Molly grimaced as she stepped through the rocks. "I scraped my ankles earlier, and once I fell down and bumped my knee. Everything was fine until this fog came in and made everything wet and damp."

"Take your time, then. It's not far."

"What's not far?"

"The *cathair*. It's a very old place, just th' spot to have our questions."

"Kah-har? How do you spell that?"

"C-A-T-H-A-I-R. When ye have a 'th' in the Gaelic, it's pronounced like an 'h' in English, without the 't.' Generally the 'ah' is a short vowel.'

"Ah?"

"First letter o' th' alphabet, ye know, ah, bee, see ... "

"Oh! A, B, C ... gotcha."

They traveled in silence for some minutes, the only sound the scuffing of Molly's shoes as she scrambled carefully over the rocks. From the mist before them a dark shape emerged like a ghost ship sailing eerily out of the fog.

Molly stopped to look. "I know this place," she murmured. "This is the ring of stones where I stopped to eat my lunch today." Climbing through the space where the outer wall had collapsed, she found her way to the inner ring of stones and sat on the flat rock where she ate her sandwich earlier. "Yes, this is the place!" She wrinkled her brow in thought, then brightened. "Ooh — I remember now! I saved my apple for later, but then I got lost. Would you like to share it with me, Paddy?" She retrieved the red fruit from her pack.

Paddy eyed the fruit with obvious interest. "An apple, is it? It's been a while since I had one o' those. If you've lost your appetite ... "

"You can just say thank you," giggled Molly. "Do you have a knife to cut it with?"

"I believe I do," said Paddy as he checked his knapsack. "Aye, this'll work." Producing a small knife, he deftly separated the apple into two equal pieces, handing one back to Molly. They sat on the rocks munching, catching the occasional juice that ran down their chins with napkins that Molly had thought to bring.

"Let's get started then, shall we?" Paddy asked as he finished his apple. Stooping down, he plucked a small blue flower that clung to the gap between the rocks. "This is Gentian. It does well here in th' Burren, but can be rare elsewhere." He jumped up to the rock beside Molly. "In th' hands of a leprechaun, the *Gentiana verna* can be used to enhance th' power o' th' firinne spell."

Molly backed away. "You never said anything about a spell."

Paddy looked at the girl over the blossom he twirled in his fingers. "Now how would I be knowin' whether th' answers to me questions are truthful unless there's a truth spell involved? I'll be castin' th' same spell on meself. There's no harm, and th' spell wears off completely in a few hours." He winked at Molly and continued, "Ye still don't understand, do ye, girl? You're in th' grand company of a magical creature! Magic is not out o' place here, it's what I am— it's what th' island is!"

Molly sighed and her shoulders relaxed. "I suppose, if it's the only way you'll show me the way home."

"That's th' girl! Now close your eyes."

"What if that's a leprechaun trick, and I won't see you when I open them again?"

"Molly, me dear, ye looked away earlier and I didn't disappear! I could have taken th' opportunity to spirit meself away then. So it's not much choice ye have here but to trust old Paddy, reliable soul that he is."

"Reliable, right," Molly snorted, but obediently closed her eyes. Paddy gently brushed the petals over her forehead, muttering some strange words, then closed his own eyes and repeated the process for himself.

If either of them had had their eyes open, they might have glimpsed a dark shape gliding soundlessly over the rocks, stopping to observe the unusual sight of a tiny leprechaun sitting with a small red-haired girl, their eyes closed tight in the mist. But then the shadow melted back into the fog, as if it had never been.

"There, ye can open your eyes, now." Paddy gave the flower one last sniff and inserted it into his pocket with the petals sticking out. Molly looked at the little man and smiled. "Thank you for staying, Paddy."

"Um— well— you're welcome," Paddy coughed. "Now, th' rules."

"There are rules?"

"O' course there's rules, you can't just go castin' a powerful spell like th' fírinne and not have rules!" Paddy held up three fingers. "First rule: Before each question, ye have to specifically say that you're askin' one o' th' seven questions. As in, and this is just for demonstration purposes, here is Question One. If ye don't specify that you're askin' one o' th' seven questions, it's just a normal question and it doesn't count."

"Okay," Molly nodded. "I can do that."

"Second rule: The spell binds ye so that ye have to tell th' truth. Neither o' us will have any choice in th' matter."

Molly grinned. "Isn't that going to be hard on you?"

"You have no idea," he grimaced. "Third rule: Ye can ask some follow-up questions after one of th' main questions, and it doesn't count as one o' th' seven questions. Even so, th' follow-up questions must be answered truthfully as well. In other words, ye can't hide th' truth by not tellin' enough of it."

"Is that it? Who goes first?"

"Age before beauty, they say, so I'll be goin' first." Paddy plumped his knapsack and lay back on it. "Question One for ye, Molly O'Malley, why are ye in Eire?"

Molly rolled her eyes. "I feel like I've told everyone on the planet why I'm here." She sighed and leaned back against the stones. "My father is a salesman. He's away on business most of the time, so it's just me and Mom at home. It's been really hard on Mom, so hard that she just got worn out and sick and couldn't do it anymore. Dad came home to take care of her, but he said he couldn't manage to take care of me, too, so he shipped me over here to spend probably the whole summer with my Aunt Shannon. She lives in Murroogh, which is where I'm trying to get back to." Molly paused and took a drink of her water. "Is that enough?"

"O'Malley is a fine Irish name. What is your father's name, then?"

"Sean. Sean O'Malley."

"And your father never brought ye to Eire before?"

"My father *hates* Ireland. He left when he was young to get a job and never came back. Now all he loves is his job."

"So you're here against your will, then?"

Molly was silent for a moment. "No, I can't truthfully say that. I'm here because my parents asked me to be here. I don't like it, I don't agree with it, but deep down, I want to please my parents."

Paddy pressed his finger tips together and nodded. "All right, then, it's your turn."

Molly sat up and looked closely at the elf. "What *is* a leprechaun?"

"A leprechaun is the smallest of angels that was accidentally left out o' heaven when God took th' heavenly host back after th' great battle with th' devil. We are th' most pure o' all God's creation, workin' tirelessly to help those who are less fortunate."

Molly thought for a second, then she smacked her head. "Oh, yeah," she said, "Question One. What is a leprechaun?"

Paddy Finegan collapsed on the ground in laughter. Tears came from his eyes as Molly looked on in amusement. "Oh, that's classic, Molly me dear, that's grand!" he wheezed. "And you figured it out so quickly! Oh, I *am* impressed!"

"Wonderful," she teased. "Can you answer the question and be impressed at the same time?"

Wiping his eyes, Paddy regained his composure. "I haven't laughed so hard in years." Looking at Molly, he took a deep breath. "Now, where were we? Ah, yes, what is a leprechaun?"

He sat up and straightened his apron. "A leprechaun, such as meself, is one o' th' fairy folk that lives in Eire. We pride ourselves on bein' excellent shoe makers" — here he presented his own foot with satisfaction— "and we make th' shoes for all those in th' fairy kingdom."

Molly examined the tiny buckled shoes in wonder. "Those are beautiful," she agreed.

"You'll not find a better cobbler anywhere than a leprechaun."

"They look very nice, Paddy. I wish I had better shoes than the ones I'm wearing. I scraped my ankles pretty good today." She rubbed the angry red patches above her sneakers. "Do all of the leprechauns look like you?"

Paddy nodded. "As much as any person looks like another. We're all about th' same height, about two feet tall, or just over half a meter. Most are older than me, and have beards. We can have black hair, red hair, brown hair, not so much blonde, but it can happen. Many o' th' leprechauns love to smoke th' pipe."

"Do you smoke?"

"Never touch th' stuff. It'll take a hundred years off o' your life." He yawned and stretched.

Molly stared at him. "How old *are* you, Paddy?"

Paddy stretched to his full height. "I'll be 400 years old next spring," he announced proudly. "I'm not as old as many, but I've been around for a few years!"

"I'd say so," Molly whistled. "Are all the leprechauns as nice as you are?"

"Leprechauns are known for their bad tempers, but that's due to th' clurichauns."

"Clurichauns? What's that?"

"It's not a what, it's who. Clurichauns are ... oh, let's say *cousins* of the leprechauns" — he winced as he said it — "who look very much like us, but behave badly. They drink too much, have surly tempers and are rude. They dress like dandies, in bright colors, but they are lazy and don't like an honest day's work. They give leprechauns a bad name."

"Well, I'm glad I met you instead of a clurichaun."

Paddy smiled. "If you'd have met a clurichaun, ye wouldn't be havin' *this* conversation, that's for sure."

Molly looked at the blue flower tucked into Paddy's apron. "Paddy, you cast a magic spell for the Seven Questions. How much magic can you do?"

Paddy shrugged. "Lots o' simple stuff, vanishing spells and th' like. We also carry two pouches. One pouch holds a silver shilling that always comes back to th' leprechaun when it's paid out. Th' other pouch holds a gold coin, which turns to dust or just vanishes after th' leprechaun who gives it away is safe. Then there's ... " he swallowed hard ... "th' wishes."

Molly leaned forward, her green eyes wide. "Wishes? You can do wishes?"

"Well, that's th' legend at any rate. Generally if we're caught, we'll promise three wishes to let us go. Most o' th' time we get away through trickery. I'm not convinced that th' wishes are real, it may just be something that leprechauns have made up over the centuries to help keep us safe."

"Oh." Molly sat back, disappointed. "Wishes. That would be so cool."

The leprechaun fixed a stern eye on the girl. "Now don't you be thinkin' that wishes are th' answer to your problems. Wishes can be nothin' but trouble. If ye don't word them right, they can cause something that ye didn't intend at all."

"I thought you said that wishes weren't real?"

"I said I didn't know for sure. There's a lot of speculation, though, and I know if I don't cast th' minor spells right, they can have problems. I can just imagine what a wish would do."

Molly nodded. "Paddy, what did you mean earlier when you said the usual approach is to never take your eyes off of a leprechaun?"

"If you take your eyes off o' a leprechaun, they can vanish in an instant. It's how we get away if we should be captured."

"Why would anyone want to capture you?"

Paddy's eyes glowed with anger. "For th' gold, girl. Have ye finished your question now?"

Molly looked at the little man in alarm. "No," she whispered. "I have to know about the leprechauns' gold first."

"I thought it would come to this. All leprechauns work hard and guard their earnings. We have our gold saved in a crock or stored in a safe place, all o' our life's savings. It's what big 'uns like ye are after, it's why they capture poor little leprechauns and try to force them to reveal where their pot o' gold is!"

"But your gold is hidden, right?"

Paddy narrowed his eyes. "After a rainstorm, th' rainbow comes out. The end of the rainbow stops over a leprechaun's pot o' gold."

"That's silly. Everyone knows that a rainbow just keeps on moving away from you as you walk toward it."

Paddy opened his eyes wide again. "Have ye ever followed a rainbow in Eire, girl?" Molly shook her head. "Have ye finished your question *now?*"

"I guess so."

"Good, because I have a question for *you.*"

Molly sighed. "And I can guess what it is."

"Question Two: Are ye after me gold?!"

chapter six

Countdown to Friendship

olly's red hair bounced as she shook her head. "It's a waste of a perfectly good question, Paddy," she said sadly. "I told you before, gold, or money, or whatever you want to call it, does nothing good if that's the main thing you're after. Look at you! A hard-working leprechaun with a crock of gold, and you're standing there all mad because you won't believe a sixth grader!"

Paddy's jaw dropped. "Then you're serious about your father chasin' th' gold and neglectin' his family?"

Molly nodded, even more sadly. "That seems to be the case." A tear tracked down her cheek, dodging freckles as it reached her chin. "I'm just caught in the middle, and now I've gotten myself lost in the Burren on top of everything else. Paddy," she wiped the tear away, "can we spend the rest of the questions getting to know each other better? I'm tired of all of this fighting."

The leprechaun sat down heavily and nodded. "I'm tired, too. It's sorry I am that I didn't believe ye. But I had to know, ye see. I had to know."

"May I ask my Second Question now?"

"Aye."

"Second Question, Paddy Finegan: Why are you so suspicious of humans?"

The elf smiled, then looked up at the girl sitting next to him. "Probably because you're not th' first one I've met."

"You've met people before? Did they try to steal your gold?"

"Aye, girl. Billy Cann left his pony to wander away so he could jump me from behind. Ah, what cruel fingers that man had! He nearly squeezed th' life out o' me! There was not a breadcrumb o' pity in that one's heart. It mattered not how much I pleaded with him that I was a poor leprechaun with barely two shillings to me name."

"Did you have more than two shillings?"

"O' course I did. But that wicked man was not about to believe th' first thing a leprechaun told him, so I told him what he was expectin' to hear. That way he was deluded into thinkin' he had th' upper hand on old Paddy!"

"What did you do?"

"Billy told me he didn't believe a word o' me story, he said that I must have a huge treasure hidden nearby, and he didn't have time for th' next rainbow to appear to show him where it was. I told him, 'It's too clever for me ye are, and as strong as a giant to boot. I've no choice but to show ye where I keep me gold. Pity, though.' I says. 'What do ye mean, pity?' Billy asks. 'Oh, just that me neighbor Eric has a crock o' gold twice th' size o' mine.' Well, Billy's eyes lit up, and he would have none o' my gold after that. He said that he could squeeze the life out o' me just as easily to get Eric's gold as he would to get me own."

"You would give up another leprechaun's gold to save your own? Paddy, I'm ashamed of you!"

Paddy chuckled. "Not a bit of it, I'd never be betrayin' a fellow leprechaun! I told Billy to carry me through the woods while I pointed th' way to Eric's gold. We came to a thick stand o' bushes, and I said, 'There in th' roots o' that center bush is where you'll find Eric's gold,' and pointed at them, and he said 'No tricks, now!' No tricks from a leprechaun, indeed!"

"Was the gold there?"

"The bushes started movin' around, and Billy turned to look at them. Then his own pony burst out o' th' bushes runnin' straight at him! He was so surprised he dropped me, and I was able to get away!"

"Wow." Molly's eyes were round with wonder. "How did his pony get in there?"

"It was his own fault. If he had taken th' time to tie her up proper instead o' lettin' her wander off, she never would have gone into th' bushes. When I pointed at th' bushes, I just bewitched her to jump out at that miserable Billy." His face softened. "That's what taught me how much humans love gold, and th' cruelty they'll stoop to to get it."

"Not at all," Molly sniffed. "It's just like I was telling you. If you let a love for gold be first, you end up doing stupid things, like forgetting to tie your pony up. If Billy had been civil, he could have been a friend to you instead of getting run over by his own horse."

"Perhaps, Molly. I've never been too trusting meself, all o' th' stories I've heard from other leprechauns are th' same story o' greed and violence. Experience only made my distrust stronger."

Molly locked her fingers together and smiled. "Well, now you're having an experience of a different sort. You'll have to think about that, too." She leaned forward. "Your turn again."

Paddy stretched and scratched his head. "Question Three, then. Why did ye come all th' way out here in th' Burren?"

Molly looked embarrassed. "I was bored. Aunt Shannon was going to be working until late, and I had finished up all of my school work. I could either look at the ocean all day, or pack a lunch and walk into the Burren."

"So ye weren't runnin' away from anything?"

Giving a sharp glance at the leprechaun, Molly continued. "I wish I could. I wish I could run away from this whole situation. I'm stuck here in Ireland, my Mom's in the hospital, my Dad's probably catching up on his work, and I can't even go for a walk without getting lost!" Her chin quivered as she spoke.

"There, there, girl. It's all right." Paddy laid his tiny hand on hers. He looked around with a smile. "I know th' Burren like th' back o' me hand."

"Is it my turn again?"

"Truly, it is."

"Question Three: What is so special about the Burren? It's just a bunch of rock, all broken up."

"That's a grand question! Many folks don't know much about th' Burren, except what they see from a distance." Paddy now wore a sly grin on his face. "Tell me, Molly, what do ye see when ye get close to th' Burren? Is it really just rocks?"

Molly cocked her head and considered. "You know, I did notice that there are lots of little plants and flowers that grow in between the rocks. Like the little blue flower you used to cast the truth spell." She gently brushed the petals still tucked into Paddy's apron. "And earlier today, I swear I saw an orchid. But it's too far away from the tropics to grow orchids out in the open!"

"Eire may be further north, but it's warm most o' th' year, with plentiful rain. The Burren is a haven for plants that normally grow in far away places, from th' Arctic to th' Mediterranean climates. Botanists from all over th' world come to th' Burren to study th' plants that grow here. By th' way, orchids can actually grow almost anywhere. What's unusual about th' Burren is that they grow on the ground instead o' high up in th' trees. We don't have many trees in th' Burren any more."

"Why not?"

Paddy frowned. "Humans again, naturally. They came and cut down th' forests, mostly to build ships. It happened centuries ago."

"Oh, I'm so sorry, Paddy," Molly said. "I imagine it would have been beautiful."

"There's still beauty here, Molly. The Burren is a giant slab of limestone, and th' weather has beaten cracks into it. Th' water runs underground, and carves out th' most wonderful caves! There are underground rivers everywhere. Limestone is a soft rock, so it forms th' caves and caverns easily. There are lots o' 'potholes' that are small openings to caves below, and some larger caves th' humans have discovered and turned into tourist attractions."

"That sounds neat. Do you go underground often?"

"It's handy if ye need a hiding place. Saves th' energy o' castin' a spell." He paused for a moment. "One last thing, th' Burren has been inhabited for thousands o' years. People have been stacking th' rocks up into monuments and tombs since before they started keepin' history. Even today, many think that they were built by fairies, so they leave them alone."

"Were they built by fairies?"

Paddy smiled. "I don't know. I'm only 400 years old, and these were built long before then. My only source would be other leprechauns, and ye can judge for yourself how reliable that might be."

Molly laughed. "That sounds fair. All right, next question!"

"Very well. Question Four: Ye don't know anything about Eire or Hibernian history?"

"I ... don't even understand that question. What is Hibernian?"

"Hibernian just means Irish. Hibernia is th' old Roman Latin word for Ireland."

"Ireland was in the Roman Empire?"

"No, but th' Romans knew about Eire. Th' Roman geographer Ptolemy listed details about Eire on his world map in the second century, with towns, rivers, tribes and th' like. There's no evidence that th' Romans ever came to Eire, but they were interested in it."

"To answer the Question, then, I don't know anything about Irish history. I learned some things during my trip over here, and Aunt Shannon told me some things, but it's mostly modern stuff."

"Many thousands o' years ago th' fairy folk lived in Eire. Life was grand, and they spent their time in ease and merriment. Then humans came to th' isle, they lived first as hunters and later began to grow crops. They became skilled in making ornaments and jewelry from gold and silver. You'll be hard pressed to find gold coins from Eire, as most were melted down to make th' beautiful jewelry."

"So you don't have any gold coins?"

"Not so many Irish gold coins, but there have been plenty o' Spanish doubloons, Turkish gold and coins dating back to when th' Vikings were raiding Eire. Most o' th' gold that humans own has been made into earrings, necklaces, broaches and bracelets. Leprechauns have collected much o' th' gold over the centuries, so we generally have a coin or two."

"What happened to all the fairy folk?"

"At first we lived in harmony with th' humans. A sect called th' druids came into th' land from very old times with th' people called th' Celts. Th' druids revered nature and protected it. They had some magic powers, for example, some of them are said to have been able to foresee th' future. But much o' their magic was knowledge of th' fairy folk, and how to avoid them and avoid conflict with them." Paddy stretched his legs out. "Th' fairy folk all live in hidin' now, as they have for many centuries since humans came. But many tales and legends still exist among humans about us. At least, what they *think* are legends."

"Cool." Molly nodded in wonder. "Can I ask my next Question now?"

"Ask away, girl."

"Question Four: What is this — kah-har where we are now? Why was it important that we come here for the Questions?"

Paddy nodded his head approvingly. "A sharp eye, and a sharp mind it is ye have, Molly! This is called a ringfort by humans. Ringforts are plentiful in Eire, and humans don't know quite what to make o' them. They were built before recorded history, so they don't know whether it was early human settlers or th' fairies themselves that built them. They don't know the purpose of th' ringforts, either."

"Is it called a ringfort because it is round, like a ring?"

"Quite so. Many think that they are magical, like a fairy ring."

"What is a fairy ring?" Molly asked.

"A fairy ring starts out as a mushroom. A mushroom grows underground, although many people don't realize that because they only see th' little mushroom umbrella when it pops above ground. As it grows, it uses up th' nutrients and spreads outward. After a while, th' nutrients are used up in th' middle, and new mushrooms grow around th' edges, formin' a circle."

Molly wrinkled her nose. "Why is it called a fairy ring, then?"

Paddy laughed. "Mushrooms pop up overnight, as if by magic. Some think that fairies dance in a circle under th' moonlight which wears out th' grass beneath their feet. Th' magic o' th' fairies lingers afterward. In fact, a fairy ring is said to be a gateway to th' fairy world."

"And this ringfort is supposed to be some kind of gateway as well? That's why it's built in a circle, too?"

Paddy nodded. "That's how th' leprechauns use them. I don't put much stock in them, like th' wishes. But it can't hurt. If it can make th' truth spell stronger, so much th' better." He scowled briefly. "Although I can't remember when I told so many true things at one time before in me life."

Molly smiled warmly. "If it makes you feel any better, Paddy, I'm glad that you're telling me the truth. Sometimes the truth can be hard, but truth between friends is a good thing."

"Well, there was no way around it." He paused. "I could have disappeared and left ye here, but somet'in' told me ... " He shook his head. "Question Five, Molly O'Malley. It's probably just th' leprechaun in me, but I have to be sure. What is th' desire of your heart?"

Molly pressed her lips together. "I guess that desires can change over time. Right now, though, my heart's desire is that my family would get back together. I want Dad to spend time with Mom and me, not just buy us stuff so he won't feel guilty. I want Mom to get better and be happy again." She smiled at the small man before her. "And maybe I can find a friend I can talk to. Paddy, are you sure this truth spell works?"

Paddy flashed a toothy grin. "Just try telling me somet'in' that isn't true."

Molly opened her mouth and paused, a look of surprise dawning on her face. She closed her mouth and shook her head as if to clear it. "Gosh. I was trying to tell you that I had a German Shepherd as a pet at home, but I just couldn't. What a strange feeling! I guess that the truth spell *does* work. Is it the same for you?"

Paddy grimaced. "Even stronger maybe, because I haven't had as much practice telling th' truth as you have."

"Does... does it hurt?"

He shook his head. "Not really. It's more a feeling o' discomfort. And th' words just never get out o' me mouth."

Molly nodded. "And then it feels so good when you do tell the truth, such a nice warm feeling. My turn again?"

Paddy nodded in agreement, and Molly continued. "Question Five. You used a spell so we would tell the truth. Are there other magic people in Ireland?"

"They're not people, actually, although some of us look sort o' like people. Leprechauns are part o' th' fairy folk, which includes fairies, sprites, pixies, goblins and several assorted spirits."

"So all of the fairy tales that my Mom used to read to me when I was little are real? They really happened?" Molly's eyes were wide.

Paddy chuckled. "I doubt that th' stories you heard were true in all th' details. Humans tell stories accordin' to what they understand, and sometimes they just make things up to make th' tale more interestin'." His voice dropped to a low whisper. "But th' stories do have a basis in fact. Fairies do exist, whether people choose to believe in them or not.

And some o' what humans have learned about us has made it into th' fairy tales."

"Do you have a leader or something? Or do you all just do whatever you want?"

"Oh, no, we have a leader, that we do," Paddy replied. "She is th' queen o' all th' fairies, and a fierce one she is. You humans may think o' all fairies as sweet gossamer things, but th' queen has great power. Cross her at your own peril, ye do."

"Does she live around here?"

"No, and I'd rather that ye didn't ask me where she *does* live. Th' leprechauns are th' queen's guards, among other things."

"I won't ask, Paddy. You took a real risk in casting that truth spell on yourself, too. I can see you take your guard duties seriously. Are there any other interesting spirits?"

Paddy swallowed and looked away across the ringfort. "Well, there's th' Banshee," he whispered.

"The Banshee? Who's he?"

"Not a he. The Banshee is a woman, a spirit who comes to wail and moan. She appears to warn humans of an impending death."

"Imm-pending?"

"That means that it's about to happen, but hasn't happened yet. The Banshee tells th' future of a doomed soul."

"How awful!" Molly hugged her knees to her chest. "She must be frightening to see!"

"Aye, her garments are all tattered and torn, and she floats on the storm that brings her. But some who have suffered with a long disease, or those who have lived a long and full life welcome th' wail o' th' Banshee."

"Well, *I'm* not ready to hear the wail of the Banshee yet! Although I wasn't sure earlier when I was lost and thought I would die."

Paddy leaned forward. "Question Six. What do ye want to do with your life?"

Molly blinked in surprise. "I'm only in sixth grade. How would I know what I want to do with my life?"

"I'm askin' what ye want to do now, girl," Paddy said gently. "I want to see where your compass is pointin'."

"My compass?"

"Surely ye know what a compass is?"

"Sure, it's a drawing tool with two legs and a hinge. You use it to make a circle."

Paddy rollicked with laughter. "Right ye are, Molly, right ye are. I meant a magnetic compass, to tell direction."

"Oh, *that* kind of compass." Molly nodded. "But I don't have a compass."

"It's a metaphor, girl. It's a picture that helps explain something that is similar. Ships used a magnetic compass to guide them when they were away from any landmarks and couldn't see th' sun or stars. The compass needle is a magnet, and it always points to th' magnetic north pole, so they could tell which direction they were going." He arranged a few blades of grass on top of a rock in a crude circle. "People have a compass o' sorts, too. There's always somet'in' that draws them, somet'in' that interests them, just like th' north magnetic pole does for a magnetic compass." He paused and looked into Molly's eyes. "What would ye *like* to do, if ye could do it?"

Molly thought for a minute, looking at the circle of grass leaves on the gray rock. "I think I would like to do something to help people. Lots of people need help sometimes, like when they get sick they need a doctor or a nurse. And kids need parents." She wiped an unexpected tear from her eye. "If I had the power, that's what I'd do, Paddy."

"Sure, and that's a grand answer," Paddy murmured, and was quiet for a moment. "What's your next Question, Molly?"

"Question Six. Aunt Shannon said that there weren't that many people in Ireland anymore. Is that true? What happened to them?"

"'Tis a sad tale and a grand one, that," Paddy sighed. "I remember in me youth many more humans living in Eire. There were about eight million souls at th' end o' th' 18th century. Life was hard enough, but then it got even harder."

"Harder? How?"

"Most o' th' peasants lived by growin' potatoes, and only potatoes. Unfortunately, they grew only one particular type o' potato. Most o' th' crop was wiped out by a blight, and there was nothin' left to eat."

"Couldn't they eat other food instead?"

"They could, if they could afford it. England ruled Eire at that time. Even durin' th' height o' th' great famine, th' English landlords sent more food from Eire than England sent back. Things like cattle, ham and bacon went to England. But th' Irish couldna afford to buy those things, and th' English government didna stop th' goods from being shipped out o' Eire."

"Did— people die?"

"Aye, they did. Between 500,000 and two million may have perished from all over Eire. I'll tell ye, I never saw so many sufferin' humans."

"Did you get hungry?"

"Ah, we leprechauns are masters at hidin' and not bein' noticed. It was simple to snatch a bit o' food from th' English landlords that were shippin' food back to their mother country."

"Paddy, that sounds like a terrible time. Why do you say that it's grand, too?"

Paddy spread his arms wide. "Many o' th' Irish had to leave and go to other countries. Millions o' them went to America, to Canada, to England and Australia. Before a century had passed, th' population in Eire had dropped to less than three million. But th' Irish took their traditions and their love o' Eire with them, and made their mark wherever they went. They worked hard, got jobs in law enforcement and politics. It's a rare thing to find someone who doesn't claim to be Irish on Saint Patrick's Day in America!"

Molly sat quietly, and Paddy looked at her with a pained expression. "Ah, I'm sorry, girl! I forgot that your father didn't bring ye up with knowin' your Irish roots an' all. Here I am going off on how th' Irish are known around th' world for their achievements, all from this grand little island, and not even thinkin' about your feelings. Can ye forgive an old leprechaun, Molly?"

Molly pushed a strand of hair back behind her ear. "It's all right, Paddy," she murmured. "It was nice hearing all of the history. It's something that I can think about — after all, my father is from Ireland, and Aunt Shannon is here, and I'm learning so much. Even if not all of the history is pretty. It's what makes Ireland, Ireland."

"You've a gift for tellin' th' truth, with or without a spell, that's for sure," Paddy said softly. "Are ye ready for me last Question, then?"

Molly sighed. "Are we to Question Seven already?"

"That we are. Question Seven— Molly O'Malley, can I trust ye?"

She looked directly into Paddy's clear blue eyes. "Paddy, I wouldn't do anything to hurt you. You know what I want, and that's *all* that I want. You're like that part of Ireland that I never knew, and now I know you, and — well, you're magic! You say you can be mean and nasty, but you've been the perfect gentleman today, and I love you for it. Yes, Paddy Finegan, you can trust me!"

Paddy stood stunned by the intensity of Molly's reply. "I did only use one flower, didn't I?" he mumbled.

Molly got to her feet and brushed herself off. "Question Seven for you, Paddy Finegan." He turned and looked up at the girl, who still dwarfed him. "Paddy, can I trust *you?*"

A smile curled his mouth, tugging at his cheeks. "I've never in me life had anyone trust me! Not in 400 years!" He turned his face up and grinned. "But I've never met th' likes o' Molly O'Malley in 400 years, either! And here you're askin' me if ye can trust me."

He put his hand on his chest. "This is so strange. Th' discomfort we talked about before, from th' spell?" Molly nodded. "I don't feel it now, Molly. It's only that nice warm feelin' that ye were talkin' about."

He picked up his knapsack, stuffed the shoe and the hammer into it, shouldered the whole works, and pivoted to face Molly. "Yes, dear girl, ye can trust ol' Paddy Finegan. Now, let's be off to find your Aunt's house before th' sun sets!"

chapter seven

Magic in the Burren

*t*he fog lifted as they cleared the ridge. Over the ocean the sun was still hanging in the sky, although it was starting to swell as it approached the horizon. Molly still had to be careful, for though the rocks were dry here, it was actually harder to find her footing going downhill than it was going up.

Soon Murroogh was clearly in sight. "There's the house!" Molly exclaimed, pointing. She turned to him with a smile. "Thank you, Paddy! It was grand spending the afternoon with you. I'll never forget it."

Paddy looked down at his buckled shoes, then up to Molly's beaming face. "I may have a bit o' trouble forgettin' it meself!" he mumbled. "Anyway, you'll be safe and sound from here. I'll be makin' me way back into th' Burren."

"Alright! Take care of yourself!" Molly waved as she turned and jogged down to the cottage.

Entering quietly through the back door, Molly found that Aunt Shannon had not yet returned from Doolin. Breathing a sigh of relief, she cleaned up and changed her clothes. She was just putting her backpack away when her aunt pulled into the driveway.

"My word, what a day!" Shannon exclaimed as she came through the front door. "It was so thick with customers we didna have a moment of peace. Course, that's good for business. How was your day, dear?"

"Oh, it was interesting." Molly opened her science textbook and pretended to read.

"Interesting? Just yesterday ya were bored out of your mind, ya said. What made today so interesting?"

"I— was reading about some of the flowers and plants in my science book. Is it true that lots of exotic flowers grow in the Burren?"

The older woman bustled around the kitchen, putting away a few things she had picked up in Doolin before coming home. "Aye, there's all sorts of odd things in the Burren. You're rather young to be takin' an interest in botany, but then ya did say you liked science. More power to ya, dear."

Molly yawned. "Aunt Shannon, would you mind if I turned in early? I'm really worn out for some reason."

"Why, no, dear, sometimes ya get more worn out just sittin' around the house doing nothing than if ya were out hiking in the Burren all day!" She tossed a grin over her shoulder.

Molly's face turned scarlet. *Does she know, or was that just a freaky coincidence?* "Uh-huh. I think you're right." Molly scurried from the room before she had to answer any more questions. *Definitely enough questions for one day!*

———

Molly slept soundly, dreaming of leprechauns hammering and stitching their shoes. Every once in a while, a winged fairy would fly by and try on a pair of the shoes. The leprechaun's shoes always seemed to fit the first time, and the fairy would fly off, singing.

"That fairy sounds just like a bird," Molly murmured sleepily. The singing continued, and Molly cracked open an eye. Sunlight peeked under her window shade. "It *is* a bird," she sighed. "How could I have mistaken a gull for a fairy?"

She stretched and tossed the covers back. "I wonder what we're having for breakfast." As she slipped out of the bed, her foot touched something just under the edge. Curious, she leaned over and looked to see what it was.

Sitting under the edge of her bed was a pair of boots. They had good, strong laces, and were made of some kind of leather. "Where did these come from?" Molly whispered, pulling them out to examine them more closely.

The leather was soft and supple, but felt like it would give good support. Holding them up to her feet, Molly decided they were about her size. "Wish I had seen these yesterday. I could have used them."

She took a quick shower and dressed. Pulling on a pair of light wool socks, she tried the boots on. They fit her perfectly. She marveled at how light they felt on her feet, and how they moved without pinching when she walked. "These are great," she whispered.

When she walked into the kitchen, she found Aunt Shannon already setting a breakfast of hot cereal and scones on the table. Shannon glanced at her in approval. "Those look nice. Did ya have those packed away in your suitcase somewhere?"

Molly gave her a blank stare. "Did I have what packed away?"

"Those new boots. They look very nice."

Molly shook her head. "I thought they belonged to you. I found them under the bed."

Shannon turned halfway around, her hand on her hip. "No, I've never seen them before. They must be yours. Do they fit ya?"

"Yes, perfectly... " Molly's voice trailed off as a thought came to her.

"There, then, ya see, ya must have just unpacked them when ya came and shoved them back under the bed. There's a logical explanation for everything, ya know." Shannon turned back to finish setting the table.

"Yes, a logical explanation for everything." Molly sat down and stared dreamily at the food.

"Are ya all right, dear?" her aunt asked as she sat down beside her. "Ya don't seem to be quite with it this morning."

"Oh, I'll be fine. Probably just got too much sleep and I had a strange dream."

"Dream? What did ya dream about?"

Molly smiled. "Leprechauns."

Shannon laughed. "Leprechauns? Now there's a bit of Irish folklore! What brought that on?"

Molly took a bite of her cereal. "Have you ever seen a leprechaun, Aunt Shannon?"

"I should say not. Not while I was awake, anyway. My mother — your grandmother — used to tell me tales of the leprechauns. But they prefer the woods and meadows, not the treeless waste of the Burren."

"But they could be in the Burren, couldn't they?"

"If they were real, I suppose they could be anywhere. They're just tales, meant to entertain children."

Molly nodded uncertainly. "Aunt Shannon? Can you tell me more about Grandma O'Malley? What happened to her and Grandpa?"

Shannon put her spoon down and held her hand to her chin. "They were driving to Dublin, and were both killed in an auto accident. They were still young, but your father and I, fortunately, were old enough to be on our own. Your dad left soon after that. I'll never forget the night before they left." She shivered with the memory. "There was a storm, and ..."

"And what, Aunt Shannon?"

"I thought I heard a woman's voice crying outside my window." Shannon smiled nervously. "Just a young girl's imagination running wild."

Molly sat up in astonishment. "The Banshee," she whispered.

"The what?"

Molly blinked and turned to her aunt. "It could have been the Banshee, warning that they would die."

"Molly O'Malley! Now who has been filling your head with such nonsense?"

Ignoring the question, Molly persisted. "Did you look out of your window? Did you see anything?"

Shannon's face turned white. "It could have been anything, there was a storm blowing things around! It was only there for a moment, like a woman in tattered clothes with the wind all around her, but it was so dark... "

Molly reached out and grasped her aunt's hand. "It's all right, Aunt Shannon, I'm sorry I upset you. Please don't be sad!"

Shannon looked at her niece in wonder. "How did ya know? How did ya know I saw something?"

"I didn't. You said you heard the woman's voice, plus there was the storm, and it all started making sense." Molly gulped. "I'm just as surprised as you are about all of this stuff."

Shannon took a deep breath. "Well, I still put it down to imagination, and you'd best do the same, or you'll be havin' nightmares instead of pleasant dreams!" She rose and began to clear the table. Molly hurried to help. Soon the kitchen was serviceable, and Shannon prepared to leave.

"I have another day at Mrs. Walsh's, and then the pub, dear. Do try not to bother your head with all of this mythical nonsense!" She kissed Molly on the forehead and swept out of the door. Molly watched through the window as the car vanished beyond the stone wall.

She sighed deeply. "I think I need to get the myth's side of this." Packing another lunch, and slipping her science book in for good measure, she left the house and headed for the Burren.

Molly's new boots made the climb much more pleasant than the previous day's. They wrapped her ankles with their protective cover, and the soles gripped the rocks without slipping. Soon she reached the ringfort.

She sat on the rock ledge where the day before she had traded questions with a *leprechaun.* "Was I out of my mind?" she said out loud. "Could I have imagined the whole thing?"

"Doubtful." The voice came from behind her. "Th' fírinne spell is far less effective on imaginary beings."

Molly spun around to find Paddy Finegan sitting placidly on a nearby perch. Today he wore a green derby hat, and his apron was gone. "Paddy!" she squealed. "You're here! You're really here!"

"Well," he said with a wink, "I was curious as to how th' new boots were workin' out."

"I knew it! I knew it was you! You made these boots for me! Oh, they're so nice, Paddy, they're wonderful! Thank you!"

He yawned and smiled in return. "I was up all night workin' on those, so I'm takin' today off. You wouldn't happen to have an apple in your pack, would ye, Molly?"

"I brought an extra, so you can have a whole one." She held it out to him. "I've been so confused this morning— I almost thought it wasn't real. Aunt Shannon was so sure... at least until she told me about the Banshee."

"Th' Banshee?"

"Aunt Shannon remembered what might have been a Banshee the night before my grandparents died. She heard a woman's voice crying outside, and when she went to look she thought she saw a woman in tattered clothes in the storm."

"Aye, it's possible. I'm sorry about your grandparents, Molly."

"They died before I was born. It must have been awfully hard on Aunt Shannon. She said my dad left soon afterward and never came back. It was probably hard on him, too."

"But now your aunt doesn't believe th' Banshee was real?"

"She doesn't believe any of this is real. Banshees, leprechauns— she thinks it's all imagination." Molly laughed. "But it's not my imagination! You're right here, and I'm wearing boots that were made by the finest leprechaun shoemaker in Eire!"

"I thank ye for that compliment, milady," Paddy boomed as he swept his derby off his head and bowed low. "Now what would ye be wantin' to do today?"

Molly smiled. "I'd like to have lunch with a friend."

Paddy smiled back. "Grand minds think alike!"

They sat on a smooth rock table, sharing apples and some delicious cheese that Paddy had brought. The sun was warm, and puffy cumulous clouds dotted the sky like cotton candy.

"I'm glad the fog is gone today," Molly observed after swallowing a bite of her sandwich. "The Burren looks a lot different when the sun is out."

Paddy looked up as the sun ducked briefly behind a passing cloud. "Aye, it looks to be a grand day. There are just enough clouds to keep th' sun off now and then, but not enough for a rainstorm."

"I brought my science book with me. I thought I could look up some of the plants and flowers that grow here." Molly patted her backpack.

"There's a lot to see here, truly. There is limestone all across th' Burren, but it's usually broken up, leaving gaps between th' rocks. Grass grows well in th' gaps, and th' Burren is actually prized as good pasture for feedin' cattle in th' winter."

"What about these deep cracks over here, Paddy?"

"Those are called grikes. They can be up to two meters deep. Ye be careful ye don't step in one o' them. Th' maidenhair fern likes to grow deep in th' grikes where th' air stays moist. Th' fern generally likes a warmer climate."

Molly thumbed through her book. "Yes, here's a picture of a fern. It says it is southern Mediterranean."

"Th' other Mediterranean plant that ye tend to find is th' dense-flowered orchid. There are many types o' orchids — some actually look like bees to attract th' real insects to th' flower."

"Why would they want to attract bees?" asked Molly.

"Do ya think that flowers have bright colors and pleasant smells just for your enjoyment?" Paddy's eyes danced. "Th' flowers use those things to get th' insects to come. Th' insects get pollen on them from the flowers, and they carry it with them to th' next flower. Some o' th' pollen rubs off o' them there, and that pollinates th' flower."

"Pawl-in-nates? What's that?"

"Th' flowers need pollen from other flowers to grow seeds to make new flowers. Without bees and insects to carry all th' pollen around between th' flowers, they would die out and we wouldn't have any flowers. Then ye wouldn't need to drag that heavy book around with ye." Paddy grinned.

"Very funny. What about the plants that normally grow where it's cold?"

"The gentian is actually one of those arctic plants. It's best known for growin' in high valleys in th' Alps. The *Dryas octopetala* ye mentioned yesterday, th' white flower with eight petals, is also an arctic variety. They grow well in th' grassy areas or where th' rock is broken into gravel."

Molly closed her book, laid back on the rock and looked up at the clouds. "This is so cool out here in the Burren, Paddy. I can't believe that I thought I would die here in the fog yesterday."

"It can be dangerous here, too, Molly. Ye were fortunate to find me or you could o' been in big trouble. Yes, it can also be beautiful." He sighed. "Many things are both beautiful and dangerous."

He looked at the sun which had started to sink lower in the sky. "I think you'd best be getting' back to your aunt's house, girl. We've been out here quite a while."

"Okay," Molly yawned. "But I still think it's cool out here."

chapter eight

The Leprechauns' Problem

Paddy walked in silence as Molly chatted merrily about how incredible the Burren was. They crossed the ridge that overlooked Galway Bay and paused to say goodbye. The leprechaun forced a smile as they parted. Molly gave him a quick hug and skipped down to the village in her new boots, humming a tune to herself. Paddy exhaled slowly then turned back into the Burren.

He seemed to walk more slowly as he made his way toward the ringfort. Changing course, he struck off in an easterly direction. Behind him, the sun extinguished itself in the Atlantic, and soon the half moon peeked over the hills, flooding the rockscape with a silvery light.

A dolmen rose above the horizon in front of him, the great top slab supported by two portal stones that raised the top high in the air. The moonlight illuminated the structure, reflecting off the light colored stone and casting dark shadows at its base. Paddy approached the place warily.

In the shadows a match flared suddenly, lighting the bearded face of wizened man the same size as Paddy. He lit a clay pipe, puffed several times to get it burning, and snuffed the match out. He stared at Paddy for a few seconds, then spoke grimly, "I'm glad ye could make it, Paddy. We've things to talk about."

Paddy found a seat across from the other leprechaun. "Howareyah, Kevin?" He looked out across the Burren. "It's a grand night out."

"I'll come right to the point, Paddy," Kevin said gruffly. "We've enough troubles without you fraternizin' with a human. It's not becomin' o' our race."

A smirk found its way to Paddy's face. "Oh, it's th' girl ye think is responsible for th' troubles, then? I have to hand it to ye, Kevin, you're a far sight wiser than old Paddy to solve it this quickly! Who'd have thought that an eleven year old girl could pull something like that off?"

"Now, ye know I don't think she has anything to do with it! Don't ye be puttin' words in me mouth! I'm just sayin' that leprechauns have never had a good relationship with the big 'uns, and we never will! They can't be trusted!" Kevin puffed furiously on his pipe, making the bowl glow like a volcano about to erupt.

"As a general rule, I'd agree with ye," Paddy nodded. "but there's no dodgin' th' firrine spell as to whether you're a threat or not."

Kevin gaped at the other leprechaun. "Ye cast the firrine on her? Whatever for? Ye know they can't be trusted!"

Paddy looked at Kevin with somber eyes. "This one can. The firrine doesn't lie. I wasn't sure meself, at first, but th' girl is no threat to us. More than that, she's under my protection. Ye leave her be, or it's me you'll be answerin' to."

Paddy stood up as Kevin stared at him, speechless. "Now," Paddy continued, "let's get on with th' real problem for tonight. Have there been any other losses?"

"Aye," said Kevin shakily, "Old man Darragh went out huntin' mushrooms two nights ago, and when he returned ..."

"The same." Paddy growled in frustration. "There were no clues, again?"

"Only the same scratch marks. No one's ever seen grooves that deep. It always happens at night. Paddy, no one knows if they'll be next! Heaven help us if we get more rain, every crock in the county will light up."

"If it rains, we'll just have to move." Paddy shook his head. "I know it's a bother, but it can't be helped. Haven't several happened without any rain first?"

"Sure, and that's what has really got the community worried. Somet'ing is trackin' without a rainbow."

Paddy leaned against the portal stone. "What about th' other counties? Are they gettin' hit, too? Howabout Donegal?"

Kevin shook his head. "Donegal is fine. It's only here in Clare, and only in the Burren." He looked at Paddy, his eyes filled with dread. "What if it spreads, Paddy? How will we stop it?"

"We don't even know what *it* is." He held his hand out of the shadow of the dolmen so that it was bathed in moonlight. "We can't fight what we can't see. This may call for desperate measures."

"Are ye suggestin' that we move, Paddy? That we give up the Burren?"

Paddy smiled bitterly. "And who's to say that it won't follow us if we move out? If we lead it to other areas, it would spread. No, we need to fight it here."

Kevin tapped his pipe out against the rock and carefully put it away. "Well, we need to find out what it is before we can fight it. None o' the others have any better ideas, either." He rose to his feet. "I'll be gettin' home, now. Paddy, you watch yourself with that girl. I hope ye know what you're doin'."

Paddy reached out and the two shook hands. "Kevin me lad, that's about the only thing that I *am* sure about right now."

The bearded leprechaun departed across the broken ground and vanished. Paddy stood gazing aimlessly after him. "Well, Paddy, ye can't be standin' around in an ancient tomb all night." He stepped out from the dolmen into the moonlight and headed to his hideaway.

Molly opened the back door and slipped into the kitchen. She was unloading her backpack when she noticed the car in the driveway. *Uh-oh.*

"Young lady, just *where* haveya been?"

Molly turned to face Aunt Shannon, who stood in the doorway to the living room, hands on her hips and looking *very* angry.

"Oh, just up on the hill a ways. The sunset is very pretty over the ocean."

"And the sunset lasts three hours, does it?"

Molly lowered her head. "Oh, you've been home for a while, then?"

Shannon nodded. "Aye. They let me off early at the pub, and I come home to find no trace of my niece, not a note, not a clue where she might be! I've been worried sick about ya!"

"I'm sorry, Aunt Shannon. I didn't mean to make you worry."

"Worry? Why would I worry about an eleven year old girl alone in the Burren?"

"I wasn't alone." Molly whispered.

Shannon went to her and grasped her shoulders. "Not alone? Who were ya with, Molly? It's no good bein' with strangers, especially at your age!"

Molly shook her head. "It wasn't a stranger. It was a friend."

"Who is it, dear? I know everyone in Murroogh."

"He's not from Murroogh."

"From Fanore, then?"

"No. He lives in the Burren somewhere."

Shannon stepped back, staring at her niece. "Come sit on the sofa, Molly. Let's have a chat."

Grudgingly Molly sat down on the worn green sofa, while her aunt took the other end. "Molly, tell me now, who is this friend you have?"

Molly sighed. "His name is Paddy Finegan."

"And how old is this Mr. Finegan?"

"400 years old. Well, next spring, anyway."

Shannon looked ready to ask another question, but was clearly too surprised to continue.

"He's super nice. You know, he made me these boots in one night?" Molly patted them lovingly. "But he doesn't trust people easily, so it would probably be pretty hard for you to meet him."

Shannon recovered somewhat. "Molly, people don't live to be 400 years old."

"He's not a person, really. He's a leprechaun."

"A— a leprechaun?" Shannon swallowed. "Well, that's very interestin' ... "

"He knows all about the flowers in the Burren, and he tells the most marvelous stories. I don't think he has many friends, though." Molly frowned. "He was surprised as anything that we could wind up being friends."

Shannon placed her hand on Molly's forehead. "What are you doing?" Molly asked, surprised. "Just checking your temperature, dear, you've been out in the sun for a few hours," the older woman murmured.

"I'm all right," Molly protested. "I feel fine. I'm really sorry I worried you, Aunt Shannon. I'll leave you a note next time."

"I don't think you should go out on the Burren for a while, dear. Let's get ya something to eat, if you're hungry, and then I think ya should rest for a while."

"But Aunt Shannon, I really don't see why... "

"Rest. That's Aunt Shannon's orders, and that's final."

Molly sighed in resignation. "Okay, but I'm going to be bored again."

————————

Several weeks passed, and Molly was anything but bored. Aunt Shannon recruited her to help at Mrs. Walsh's setting tables and serving breakfast, then changing the linens later in the day. Aunt Shannon was fair about it, giving her a modest allowance for her work. When Shannon left for the pub in Doolin, however, Molly was dropped off at the house with strict instructions to stay inside.

Late one night Aunt Shannon came in fairly bouncing. "Molly, I stopped at the activity center in Doolin and checked my email."

"You have email?" Molly gaped.

"Well, I don't check it often because they charge for it at the center, but I got an email from your father. I printed it off for ya."

Molly grabbed the paper and devoured it with her eyes. She read it through a second time. "Aunt Shannon? He says that Mom is getting better, but she still needs more rest. And he asked how you were holding up with two jobs... he didn't ask about me."

"Oh, I think he asked how ya were doin' with your schoolwork, didn't he now?"

"That's not the same thing. He's still talking about things. He hasn't changed." She tossed the paper onto her bed.

Shannon sat down in the chair. "Molly, dear, I sent a reply to him while I was there. I told him how proud I was thatcha were helping out at Mrs. Walsh's, what a fine young lady you're growin' into. I told him that he should be proud of ya, too." She sighed and brushed her dark bangs back. "Your father can be difficult to talk to. All we can do is keep talking to him and keep sharing with him. Do ya know what I mean?"

Molly nodded. "It's just so hard, Aunt Shannon."

"I know, dear. Try to get some sleep."

Molly sat on her bed for a while, doodling tic-tac-toe games on the back of the email. The sun had set, and Aunt Shannon had gone to her bedroom, but Molly wasn't sleepy yet.

Tap.

Molly looked disinterestedly at the window, then returned to her doodling.

Tap.

Curious, she crawled over to the window. Looking outside, she could see nothing unusual.

Then a small face pressed itself to the pane.

"Oh! Paddy!" she whispered, and opened the window. Paddy tumbled soundlessly into the room and rolled to his feet. Looking around, he held a finger to his lips. Molly nodded. He came close and whispered, "Is your Aunt asleep?"

"I don't know. She's gone to her room, that's all I know."

"Molly, come with me. I have to talk with ye."

"Now?"

"Yes, now!"

"Just a second. I have to write a note so she won't worry if she gets up and finds me gone." She scribbled a hasty message on her tic-tac-toe paper and left it on her pillowcase.

The pair slipped out the window and walked quickly to the outskirts of the village, stopping in a grove of trees. "This'll do," the leprechaun whispered, "I know ye don't have enough time to go further into th' Burren to talk."

"Paddy, I'm sorry," Molly began, "Aunt Shannon thinks that I'm wacko or something. She's been making me help out at the bed and breakfast and stay around the house. She's not letting me go to the Burren anymore."

Paddy grinned. "There's some that think I'm a bit touched as well! But it's good to see ye, Molly, truly it is!"

Molly smiled. "What is this all about, Paddy?"

"Well ... here." He thrust his hand out to her. Silver flashed between his fingers.

"Paddy, this is ... really neat." Molly accepted the silver colored bracelet from him and examined it in the moonlight. She traced its surface with her finger. "There are shapes etched into this — like a crescent moon, and some ivy or something."

"There are more than pretty pictures etched into it. I've spent several nights getting th' enchantment just right for ye."

"What enchantment?"

"I thought it might be easier ... if ye had something that would help ... ye know, if ye needed to find me ..." Paddy turned away.

"Paddy, it's beautiful. Not only that, it's a beautiful thought, and very practical of you, too. How do I use it to find you?"

The elf smiled. "That's th' easy part. Just rub or tap th' bracelet, and say me name. I'll be able to tell where ye are."

"Okay." Molly turned the bracelet over in her hands before slipping it onto her wrist. "Paddy, you're fidgeting. Is there something else you wanted to say?"

His face darkened, and he nodded. "I want to get your opinion on somet'in'."

"What?"

"Somet'in' is happenin' out in th' Burren. Somet'in' strange. It's not somet'in' th' leprechauns are makin' any progress figurin' out, so I t'ought ..."

"You thought you'd see if there's anything that humans may know about it?"

Paddy looked down at his feet. "Well... yeah."

Molly sat down and tapped her cheek with her finger. "I don't know, Paddy, but maybe you'd better start out by telling me what you *do* know."

"Very well, then." Paddy folded his hands together and took a deep breath. "Th' leprechauns have a problem."

Molly nodded. "Go on."

"For th' past several years, somet'in' has been stealin' from us."

"Stealing what?"

"Gold." Paddy gulped and pressed on. "Gold, taken from one leprechaun after another. Th' thief strikes at night, and th' only clues left behind are deep scratch marks."

"But I thought that leprechauns' gold would vanish after being taken away."

"Only if th' leprechaun gives it away. This gold is bein' taken without th' owner's consent." He shook his head sadly.

"There's no one that knows who— or what— th' thief might be."

"Well— could you put a spell on the gold so you could track it after the thief takes it?"

"Enchant th' gold?" Paddy furrowed his brow. "Then what would keep other leprechauns from knowin' where your gold was and helpin' themselves?"

"Um... honesty?" Molly offered.

Paddy raised an eyebrow. "These are leprechauns we're talkin' about here, Molly."

"Well, it sounds like this crisis has brought the leprechauns closer together, whether you trust each other yet or not."

"We don't. But we're talkin' more to each other, a rare thing for leprechauns. And we're talkin' to our kin all over Eire, just to make sure this isn't spreadin'.."

"You mean it's only happening here?"

"Aye, in th' Burren. And worse ... "

"Worse?" Molly prodded.

"Worse, whoever is takin' th' gold isn't needin' a rainbow to find it."

"You mean the rainbow that you told me shows where the pot of gold is at the end? You know, Paddy, I still don't believe that."

Paddy chuckled. "I wonder how many people would believe ye if ye told 'em ye were talkin' to a leprechaun! It's not like the days when the great stories were shared and remembered. Everyt'ing is modern now."

Molly nodded. "I think that's what happened with Aunt Shannon. She acted like I was sick or had a fever or something when I said I was friends with a leprechaun. At least I didn't have to come up with another explanation for where I had been."

"I wish I could come up with an explanation o' where th' gold is vanishin' to," Paddy said as he shook his head sadly.

Molly's eyes brightened. "Well, why not? Paddy, did you hear what you just said? *I wish I could come up with an explanation of where the gold is vanishing to.* Why don't you make a wish? Leprechauns can do that, right?"

Paddy shook his head again. "A leprechaun can't grant a wish to himself. He can't even grant a wish to another leprechaun. He can only grant them to humans, but that's generally a trick used to get away from them."

"Oh." Molly sat down on a convenient moss-covered rock.

Paddy continued to frown, however, and his eyes glistened with new life. He shook his head slightly as if to banish the thought, but continued to ponder.

Molly plucked a blade of grass and twirled it in her fingers. She stared closely at it as it spun back and forth. "You know, Paddy," she finally said, "You've got another problem once you figure out who the thief is. If the leprechauns are half as clever as you say, I've no doubt you will figure that part out, especially since you're working together now. But after that, how will you get the thief to stop? Who are the cops of the fairy world?"

"Mmm? Oh, we are, strictly speakin'. Th' leprechauns, I mean. But as this is a leprechaun problem, we're pretty much on our own." He frowned more deeply. "But I wouldn't go so far as to say th' leprechauns are workin' together. We're sharin' information, sure enough, but that's about th' most of it."

Molly dropped the blade of grass and hugged her knees. "That's too bad. I wish you all could be friends like you and I are."

"Aye, we're truly friends, aren't we Molly?" Paddy looked away quickly.

Staring at the little man, Molly said, "Paddy ... you're not acting like yourself. We are friends ... aren't we?"

Paddy whirled around to face her, pain etched on his face. "Would a friend ask a friend for a hard favor? It's been bouncin' around in me head, but I'll not put this on ye!"

"I think a friend would ask a friend for a hard favor, if it was important. That's what friends do, they help each other out. What are you thinking about, Paddy?"

He bent his head down and pressed his hands to his temples. "I've been t'inkin' about th' wishes. But it's too much to ask."

"Paddy," Molly gently touched his shoulder. "I thought you said you couldn't use the wishes, that you couldn't grant them."

Paddy looked up at Molly, his eyes burning. "Not to a leprechaun, I said."

Molly withdrew her hand as if she had touched a hot kettle. "Oh," she said in surprise, "you mean ... "

"I won't ask it, Molly dear. I won't ask ye to accept wishes and use them to help th' leprechauns. I couldn't live with meself!"

"Well," Molly gulped, "what if I asked you, instead? 'Cause I'm certainly not going to catch you and force you to give me the wishes. You need help, Paddy, and this sounds like the best way to get to the bottom of this."

Paddy stared at her in wonder. "You'd do that? You'd take th' wishes and use them to help us, even though ye know just one of us?"

Molly made an 'X' across her chest with her finger. "Cross my heart," she said solemnly. "That one leprechaun is pretty special to me."

Paddy stared down toward the village. "Right, then." He rose to his feet. "This will take some work. Ye know th' grassy part of the hill before it starts gettin' broken up by th' rocks?"

Molly nodded.

"Meet me there at midnight tomorrow. No, make it half eleven. Can ye do that?"

"I'll try, Aunt Shannon is a pretty sound sleeper. Eleven-thirty, then. Shall I bring a flashlight?"

"You'll probably need it to find your footing in th' dark, even though th' moon will be full. Be sure not to be late. And wear your boots."

Molly grinned. "I wouldn't think of leaving them behind!"

chapter nine

Three Wishes

All of the next day Molly tried to keep her mind off of what would happen that evening. After getting home from Mrs. Walsh's, she cleaned her bathroom, made three peanut butter and jelly sandwiches and even did some of the even-numbered word problems from her math book.

It didn't help. She could think of nothing except what was about to happen up in the Burren just before midnight. Exhausted, she threw herself on to the sofa, which is where her aunt found her upon returning from Doolin.

"Had a rough day, dear?"

Molly sighed and did not rise. Her arm was cast randomly over her eyes. "Oh, I'm okay. Just running out of things to do, I guess."

Shannon smiled as she set her purse on the table. "Well, don't give up hope. I'm taking a few days off next week to take ya on holiday, show ya some of the sights here in Eire. That'll give ya something to do."

Molly uncovered her eyes. "Can you afford to take off like that? Working two jobs and all, I mean."

"Your father, generous soul that he is," she gave Molly a quick wink, "has sent me a check and a note saying to show ya a good time. He further urges that I use a bit for myself as your personal tour guide." She posed in front of the hall mirror. "Do ya think I need a new uniform for the part, dear?"

Molly collapsed with laughter. "It probably would be easier to find you if you had a new sweater!"

Shannon sat down on the sofa and gave Molly a quick squeeze. "It'll be grand, just us girls, won't it?"

They talked for a while longer before going to bed. Molly waited until she thought her aunt was asleep, and then crept out the door with her flashlight. The wind coming from the bay was crisp and cool, prompting Molly to pull her jacket tight around her.

She picked her way along the path up the hill, using her flashlight as little as possible. When she came to the grassy place one of the stones stood up and tipped his top hat.

"Paddy?" Molly whispered. She shined her flashlight briefly on him, revealing an elegant green waistcoat that sparkled in the light, fine green trousers, and a new pair of shoes with gleaming buckles.

"Where did you get that hat?" she asked. "That buckle on it is bigger than you are! I hope I don't offend you, but you look like a clurichaun in that outfit."

Paddy placed the hat jauntily on his head. "Me finest outfit for th' ultimate spell. Figured it couldn't hurt, and if it doesn't work ... " he shrugged, "at least I look grand for th' evening."

"What happens now?"

"Come sit on this stone beside me. You're just on time, good girl!"

Molly walked to the flat stone that was surrounded by a soft grassy carpet for twenty feet in each direction. She sat down at the edge and switched her flashlight off.

"Look now, just over that rise– they're comin'!" The leprechaun pointed above them.

Faintly at first, one after another a flock of tiny fireflies floated over the hill. They danced in the moonlight, spinning in circles around each other before once again moving toward the two figures on the stone.

As they drew nearer, Molly realized they were not fireflies at all, they were much too big for that. The light from each one made it too bright to look at the center clearly, but she could just make out a tiny, human-like form there, with gossamer wings that moved almost too fast to see.

"Paddy... are those ... ?"

"Shh. Yes, fairies, from th' north. Quiet now, while they do their work."

The fairies descended, touching down lightly on the grass surrounding Molly and Paddy. Scarce had they brushed the grass when they were back in the air, whirling and swirling in a delicate dance of glowing lights.

Molly could see that their dance took them in a circle about ten feet away from her. Around and around they flitted, dipping to kiss the soft grass and flinging themselves high the next instant.

Soon the dancers accelerated to a maddening speed, darting up and down and around and around. The glow of their combined light reflected off of Paddy's eyes, and he smiled with delight as the fairies cavorted.

Then in a sudden burst of bluish light, the fairies vanished, leaving Molly and Paddy in the darkness. But not quite the darkness.

Where the fairies had traced their otherworldly dance, a thin blue line shone in the night, encircling the two friends.

"Ah," Paddy breathed, "now's th' time."

He stood on the stone and stretched out his arms. "Molly O'Malley! You've captured this leprechaun's heart more surely than any bag or trap could hold th' rest o' me. And you've asked not for wishes to satisfy your greed or lust for power, but to help th' little folk.

"Therefore, by th' power o' this leprechaun, Paddy Finegan, and by th' power within this fairy circle, I bestow three wishes upon ye, Molly O'Malley!"

He produced a shamrock that had been tucked into the band on his hat and laid it gently in Molly's hand. It glowed of its own accord for a moment, the same blue of the fairy circle, then returned to its normal appearance.

Paddy sat down and breathed a sigh of relief. "Well, I've done it. As nearly as I can tell, anyway." He looked up at Molly. "Keep th' shamrock safe, and don't be blurtin' out any wishes accidentally, or you'll waste 'em. And mind ye t'ink carefully what ye *do* wish for."

The moonlight drenched them from overhead, and Molly realized the spell must have been cast exactly at midnight. The fairy circle had vanished completely, its power consumed by the wishes spell.

"So what do we do now?" Molly asked, trembling.

"We make a wish. Or more precisely, you make a wish. We need to find what is takin' th' leprechauns' gold."

"Okay," Molly exhaled, "not too many ways to say that. Here goes. I wish to find who or what is taking the leprechauns' gold."

The shamrock in Molly's palm burst into life with a blaze of green light. The light floated from her hand and stopped about three feet away where it formed itself into a glowing orb about ten inches across.

"Wait a second," Molly said, and she flipped open the heart shaped locket around her neck. Her parents shone back at her briefly in the moonlight. She dropped the shamrock into the case and snapped it shut. "Perfect fit," she announced, and turned her attention again to the orb. It pulsed slightly, like a thing alive.

"Cool," murmured Molly, "but what now?"

As if in answer, the orb began to move slowly up the hill. Molly and Paddy followed, finding that the orb moved no faster than they could climb. The green light seemed to choose the easiest path across the broken landscape, for they moved quickly and surely without incident. Then as suddenly as it had appeared, the glowing orb stopped, hovered for a moment, sank to the ground and disappeared.

Molly stood in shocked silence. "That's all? It leads us out here and then goes away?"

"Patience, girl. Let me take a closer look." Paddy bent down to examine the spot where the orb had vanished. "Bring your torch, Molly, and point it here."

Molly turned her flashlight on the spot Paddy indicated. Thick heather lay over the ground. "I wonder," Paddy muttered, and he pushed the heather aside to reveal a hole almost three feet across.

"What is it?" Molly asked.

"A pothole. Th' Burren is made o' soft limestone, and th' water beats its way around and through th' rocks. There are underground rivers here that have carved caves beneath th' surface. A pothole is a small opening that leads underground."

He peered into the hole. "Our green friend is waitin' for us, just inside."

Molly gaped at him. "You want me to go down *there?*"

"No, th' floatin' light wants ye to go down there. Ye wished to know who or what is stealin' th' gold, and this seems to be th' only way to find out."

She took a deep breath. "I should have listened when you warned me about wishes. Well, it's too late to back out now." Carefully she shined her flashlight into the hole. "It looks like there are plenty of handholds, and it slopes pretty good; at least it doesn't go straight down. I think we can make it from what I can see from here."

Molly lowered herself into the pothole, finding that the orb's light was enough to show the way. She pocketed the flashlight leaving her hands free for climbing.

Again the orb moved no faster than Molly could follow. The passage widened as they went deeper. After a short descent they came to a rock shelf with a low ceiling. The orb hovered briefly, showing a rather steep drop off, and then floated across a much larger space in the cave.

"What is it doing?" Molly whispered as Paddy came up beside her. "I can't follow across there! It's a cliff!"

Her whispers stopped as the orb began to illuminate the far side of the cave. Sparkles of light reflected back through the darkness. "Well, I'll be ... " Paddy whispered. "If that doesn't look like ... "

The subdued green light danced off a sizeable pile of gold. Coins, jewelry, and even a few ingots glowed in the orb's luminance. "Wow," Molly murmured in awe. "You leprechauns know how to save up."

Paddy shook his head. "Somet'in's wrong here," he growled. "Look at th' pile. Th' sides reflect th' light, but where th' top should be, there's nuttin' but black."

"You're right," Molly agreed. "I wonder why it does that?" She took out her flashlight. "Let's put a little light on the subject."

The flashlight's beam sliced through the cavern, reflecting the gold brilliantly. She moved the light higher to where the gold didn't seem to reflect back. Abruptly the gold stopped and there was only blackness, even with the flashlight's illumination. She moved the beam even higher.

"What's that?" Paddy asked. "A blue line? What *is* that?"

Slowly Molly moved the beam up until she could see the cave wall again. There was no doubt now, whatever it was, the black was a shape and not just darkness. She brought the beam down and to the right, pausing at an irregularly shaped area. "Still can't make it out," Molly whispered.

Unexpectedly, the orb flared brightly to illuminate the large cavern. The shape stirred, and a long, serpentine tail uncoiled to the left. In the midsection two giant wings unfolded, like those of a huge bat. Cruel black talons were now visible under the beast's strong, yet graceful legs. The great head, framed by frills on each side, lifted, and two yellow eyes reflected back the light from Molly's flashlight. A voice, raspy but strong echoed across the cavern. A thought burrowed its way into Molly's mind. A single word: *Intruders.*

"Molly," Paddy whispered. "Time to go, dear."

The green orb vanished in a final pop of light leaving the cavern in darkness except for Molly's flashlight. "Coming," Molly whispered, turning her light back to the passage they had entered from.

The pair scrambled quickly back up the tunnel with Molly leading the way. Despite the coolness of the cave Molly felt the air behind her becoming warmer.

"Hurry, Molly me dear," Paddy said with an edge to his voice.

"What's the hurry, Paddy? That thing is too big to follow us through here."

"Trust me on this, girl. It doesn't have to follow us. Quick as ye can, now!"

Stars appeared above as they neared the opening to the pothole. The walls of the passage were amazingly light around them. Molly reached the top and climbed out. She reached down for Paddy's hand, and was surprised how very bright it was below him. A sound like a waterfall rushing up the passageway grew louder and louder.

"Pull me out now, girl!" Paddy cried in desperation. Molly yanked and the leprechaun rose clear of the pothole. He dived away from the opening, taking Molly with him.

A blast of heat struck Molly as they fell. She looked at the pothole, and a fountain of flames erupted from it. As she stared the flames ceased and the glow from the pothole faded into blackness again.

"Paddy," she said slowly, "What was that?"

He sighed, brushing a bit of dirt from his fine suit. "*That* was a gold-stealing, fire-breathing, dragon."

"But," Molly protested, "I didn't think dragons were real."

Paddy's laughter rang across the hillside. "Not real, then? And you're sittin' here tryin' to convince a leprechaun?!"

"Okay," Molly said, smiling at the humor, "it *is* a dragon. At least we found out who was taking your gold."

chapter ten

Problem Solving

Molly returned to her aunt's house and slipped in the back, unnoticed as far as she could tell. She changed into pajamas and slid quietly into bed with a sigh of relief. She lay still but didn't fall asleep.

How can I sleep after almost being roasted by a dragon? A dragon, for gosh sakes...

Molly closed her eyes and pulled her blanket up over her head. She couldn't shut out the image of the flames bursting up out of the pothole. The pothole where she and Paddy had been only moments before.

"Molly?"

Molly groaned and opened her eyes. Aunt Shannon was turning off her alarm clock which was still playing the morning radio show.

"Molly, dear, your alarm went off twenty minutes ago. Didn't ya hear it, then?"

"I guess not," Molly yawned. "I was having some bad dreams and didn't sleep very well."

"Oh, look at those eyes ... ya don't look as if ya slept a wink, now. Never you mind about going to the bed and breakfast today, you stay home — and I mean stay *home*— and get some rest. You'll be no good to Mrs. Walsh in that condition."

Molly's heart jumped, but she tried to look convincingly tired. "If you say so, Aunt Shannon."

A half hour later Shannon left for the bed and breakfast. Three hours later Molly woke up again. "Wow, I really *was* tired," she groaned, rubbing her eyes. "I can't be doing that every night."

She showered, brushed her teeth and hair, pulled on jeans and a tee shirt, and then headed to the kitchen for breakfast. "No, I guess it's brunch, now, isn't it? That means I can have some of this leftover breakfast bacon *and* an orange soda." She grinned as she realized she had figured out a way around the unwritten rule about what you couldn't have for breakfast or lunch.

"Now, if only I could find a way to meet with Paddy and talk with him about the black dragon," she mumbled through a mouthful of brown bread and marmalade. She wracked her brain for a solution. Reaching for her soda, she heard a *clink* sound. Glancing down, she realized her silver bracelet had struck the edge of her plate.

The bracelet! Wiping her mouth on her napkin, she raced from the table to her bedroom and began tapping the bracelet quickly. "Paddy, Paddy, if you can hear me, I can't come out to the Burren right now. Is there any way you can come here?"

The minutes stretched into a half hour. Sighing dejectedly, Molly went back to the kitchen and cleaned up the dishes. She plopped into the big chair in the living room. "No television, no computer," she muttered. "Aunt Shannon doesn't have time for any of that. Well, I do. At least when I'm not trying to get rid of fire-breathing dragons."

Her eyes were starting to droop again when she heard a *tap* on her bedroom window. Instantly she was awake, running to her bedroom. She slid open the window and looked out. "Nothing," she murmured. "I could have sworn I heard a tap on the window."

"Leave th' window open for a second, and step back!" a familiar voice whispered.

Molly did so, and a long, slender animal jumped onto the sill. It had a furry light brown upper coat with a white underbelly. Its tail was as long as its body, and the tail was as black on the tip as if it had been dipped in ink. The creature looked quickly around the room, then dropped to the floor and ran under the bed.

"Whoa, you can't come in here!" Molly yelled, and slammed the bedroom door so it couldn't escape.

"But ye invited me in sure enough, didn't ye girl?" said the familiar voice, this time from under the bed.

"Paddy?" Molly got down on her knees to look.

Paddy Finegan lay under the bed on his stomach, his chin propped up by his hands, and his legs bent at the knees. An impish grin splashed across his face.

"Paddy, was that you? You gave me a fright! I thought Aunt Shannon would come back and we'd have some wild animal in the house ... "

"And ye t'ought she'd rather come back to find a leprechaun in th' house?"

"Come out from under there, you big dope!" Molly extended a hand and Paddy slid easily from under the bed. "What was that you turned yourself into?"

"Weasel. European, o' course. Best close that window, girl, voices can carry, especially when you're yellin' at innocent little ... " his voice dropped to a whisper – "leprechauns."

"I agree," Molly said quietly, closing the sash. "What possessed you to look like a weasel?"

"Somehow, I got it into me head," he looked severely at the red-haired girl, "that people might find it odd to see a leprechaun running across their backyards in th' middle o' th' day. But a weasel, now, maybe that wouldn't attract so much attention. What were ye t'inkin', contactin' me in broad daylight?"

"The good news is that Aunt Shannon kept me from going to the bed and breakfast this morning because I was so tired from being up most of last night. The bad news is that she grounded me from leaving the house. The only thing I could think to do was to have you come to me, somehow." She yawned and smiled faintly. "And here you are."

Paddy smiled back. "Sure, and leprechauns don't just sneak around at night! We know how to hide and disguise ourselves during th' day as well. Still, even big folk might t'ink it strange if they noticed a weasel jumpin' into your bedroom window."

Molly nodded. "It's a chance we had to take today. We need to figure out what to do about the dragon."

"First t'ings first. What door does your Aunt come through when she comes home?"

"The front, but ... "

Paddy was already running into the foyer. He listened at the front door intently. He rapped the door sharply, twice. An answering pair of knocks immediately echoed back from the wood.

"How ... " Molly began, but Paddy simply held a finger to his lips.

"Let's talk back in your room. Everyt'ing's set here!" He sauntered back across the house and jumped up to the edge of the bed, where he sat dangling his buckled shoes.

Molly closed the door behind her. "We can talk now?"

"We can talk. If ye can stay awake long enough!" Paddy winked at her.

Pulling up the lone chair in the room, Molly sat down facing the leprechaun. "I needed my sleep. You've probably been asleep for centuries if you add it all up!"

"Aye, that's probably true," Paddy said with admiration on his face. "You're quick with numbers, Molly! Let's put our talents together and see what we can come up with."

"All right," Molly began, "There's the brute force approach. We can light firecrackers and drop them down the hole. Somehow, though, I don't think that will be enough to even startle that dragon."

"How about makin' th' cave collapse to crush th' creature?"

"Um— I'm not sure that would be a good idea. Even if you killed the dragon, it would make it very hard to get the gold out afterward."

"That's true," Paddy sighed.

"How about this?" Molly said brightly. "Humans were good at hunting dragons before, at least if you believe the tales of knights and dragons. They must be even better now. Could we trick someone into getting rid of the dragon? Maybe the army, as a public safety issue?"

Paddy thought for a second. "I don't t'ink that would work either. Even if they got rid o' th' dragon, they would just keep th' gold for themselves."

"You're right. They would put it in whatever the Irish equivalent of Fort Knox is."

Four knocks sounded sharply from across the hallway. Paddy's face tightened. "It's your aunt come home, or someone at th' front door! Hide!" He dove under the bed. Molly quickly turned the chair around and jumped into the bed, pulling the sheets over her.

A key turned in the front door lock.

"Molly?" Shannon called.

"In here," Molly called back, trying to keep the tremor out of her voice.

Shannon pushed the door open and smiled at her niece. "Are ya feelin' better yet, dear? Decided I'd pop in and see how you're doing before I left for Doolin. I would have thought you'd be up and around by now!"

Molly pretended to yawn. "I think I got up too soon. I just laid back down for a nap."

Shannon shook her head. "And here I t'ought naps were only for the very young and people my age." She walked over and sat down on the edge of Molly's bed. Molly tried not to gasp.

"Mrs. Walsh has been very happy with your work at the bed and breakfast. She was concerned thatcha were so tired this morning, and was glad that I had ya stay home to rest. She also thinks that you've been workin' too hard for a child your age. And I agree."

Molly nodded, and prayed that Paddy wouldn't sneeze.

"Molly, I was worried when ya were talkin' about leprechauns and the like, and going out in the Burren by yourself. I wanted to keep ya busy, to give ya somet'ing else to do. Do ya understand me, Molly?"

Molly swallowed and tried not to let her eyes wander to the edge of the bed. "Yes, Aunt Shannon."

"I think that we need to do somet'ing together, then. Mrs. Walsh has given me tomorrow off. Do you know what we're goin' to do tomorrow?"

"Play dominos?"

"No, silly," Shannon laughed, "we're going to see Aillwee Cave! I still have to go to Doolin later tomorrow, but we can run over in the morning."

Molly felt her heart jump into her throat. "A ... a cave?"

"One of the finest in the Burren! There's another in Doolin, it's grand too, but I have a discount to Aillwee."

Molly stared at the wall. "A cave... "

"Molly, are ya listening? It's got a few places where ya have to duck— well, I do, anyway— and it has rooms in it big enough to hold ... "

"A dragon." Molly whispered.

"A dragon? Well, I suppose, if such a t'ing could exist. I don't know how it would get in there, though. What brought that up?"

"Uh, oh, I don't know. I think it was that dream I had." She blushed scarlet at the fib and looked away from her aunt.

"Molly O'Malley! You're acting so strange! You'd t'ink ya were hiding a leprechaun under the bed!"

Molly's face turned ashen as she looked at her aunt. "N-no, Aunt Shannon, really... "

Shannon hugged her niece tightly. "It's all right, dear! I'm sorry, I was just teasing ya! There's no more chance of that than there is of finding a dragon in a cave!"

Molly's eyes widened and she was glad that Aunt Shannon couldn't see them just then.

"Next T'ursday, then, I have a full holiday from both Mrs. Walsh and the pub. We'll take five days to give ya a proper tour of southwest Eire. How does that sound?" She stepped back and looked at Molly. "And don't fret about the cave. It's really all right!"

Glancing at her watch, she said, "I'd better be on the road to Doolin now. I'll see you later tonight, dear!" She turned and left the way she had come. Molly listened for the front door to shut and lock, heard the car start, and heard the gravel crunch as the car rolled down the driveway.

"Are ye sure she's just teasin', then?" came a voice from under the bed.

"Spooky, isn't it?" replied Molly.

chapter eleven

Aillwee Cave

unt Shannon let Molly sleep late the next morning, as Aillwee Cave was not far away. When they rose, they had a leisurely breakfast. Molly picked at her food, as she was still concerned about what could be done to solve the problem of the leprechauns' gold. She also felt guilty about letting the leprechauns' problem almost make her forget about her own family problems. After all, it was her dad's fault that she was over in Ireland in the first place.

"Molly, is my cookin' that bad, now?"

Molly looked up from her daydreams. "Oh, no, it's delicious, Aunt Shannon! I'm just thinking about stuff."

"Well you'd best start t'inkin' about getting some more of those eggs and bacon down ya, or you'll be runnin' out of energy before lunchtime! Would ya like some more tea, dear?"

They drove north from Murroogh along the coastal highway. The clouds hung low in the sky, dark and menacing above the waves. Broken rocks surrounded the road as they approached a tight curve to the right, revealing a small white lighthouse on the shore.

"Black Head," Shannon announced. "We turn east from here along the Bay."

Molly had a lovely view out of her left side window across to County Galway. "How far is it to the other side of the bay from here, Aunt Shannon?"

"About 16 kilometers, I reckon. Oh, I keep forgettin'— ten miles in American. We'll be comin' up on Ballyvaughan soon, it's not far."

Stone walls flanked the narrow road, but Shannon was clearly an expert at not getting squeezed by cars coming the other way, even when a large tour bus came along. Molly was glad she was sitting on the far side of the car as they passed the travelers going the other direction, although it meant that she was staring at a stone wall that looked like it was mere inches away from her window at times.

After twenty minutes they reached Ballyvaughan. It was larger than Murroogh or even Fanore. Molly didn't have much time to look at it, though, as Shannon turned right down N67 and soon after that made a left down the R480. Signs pointing the way to Aillwee Cave were plentiful, each marked with the distinctive outline of a bear. They pulled up to the main entrance from the highway just as raindrops began to sprinkle the windshield.

"Good morning," the attendant greeted them. "Good morning," Shannon replied, handing over her discount coupon and some Euros. The attendant handed some papers back and waved them ahead.

As they passed a building with a sign that read 'Farm House' it started to rain very hard. Their lane turned into a one-way road that corkscrewed steeply up the mountain. The little car's motor whined noisily in protest as Shannon shifted to a lower gear and tromped the gas pedal. Then they popped onto a level road leading to several connected parking lots. Sheets of rain pounded the car and made it hard to see.

Shannon drove slowly through the parking lots until they saw a stone building at the far end. They parked as close as they could, then sprinted for the building, ducking low under their umbrellas.

Shaking droplets from their umbrellas, the pair found themselves in a gift shop with a small café. A small door to the side marked the entrance to the cave.

"Oh, I remember now," said Shannon. "We have to trade our receipt for a token to get on a tour." She motioned at the rain-drenched patio outside the door. Molly could see a fast food counter and a ticket booth on the other side. "I'll get the tokens, dear, look around here for a bit. There's no sense in both of us gettin' wet."

Molly wandered around the gift shop, looking at jewelry. She stroked her silver bracelet gently. *These are nice, but I like my bracelet better.*

Her aunt returned with two disks that looked like CDs, but were made of wood and painted a cheerful yellow. "We're all set, then. They will call our group by color. It should be about 15 minutes."

They looked at tee shirts and figurines together. "See anyt'ing ya like, Molly?"

Molly shook her head. "I'm not really in the mood for shopping right now."

"That's all right. We'll have lots of time for souvenir hunting when we take our long trip later this week. Just wait until ya see somet'ing that ya can't live without."

Soon the yellow group was called, and they lined up to enter the cave. A young woman greeted them. "Hi, I'm Amy, and I will be your guide today into Aillwee Cave. Please step inside and stop at the next door."

Molly and Shannon walked down a narrow rock tunnel until they reached an imposing wooden door. A display hung on the wall showing a map of the cave. The left side showed a loop colored in red, and the right side showed an outline that was mostly white, with a couple of parts colored in blue. Molly wondered what it meant.

Amy came up to the front. "Have I gotten everyone's yellow disc? Great. Welcome to Aillwee cave. Again, my name is Amy, and I will be your guide. We will be walking about a third of a mile today. This map ... " she indicated the display that Molly had been looking at, "shows the cave tunnels. An underground river once flowed here and hollowed out the tunnel where we are standing. Later the water level dropped, allowing us to walk through the cave. The tour will cover everything that you see in red. This second red tunnel that loops back to the entrance is man-made, and was built to make it easier for visitors to walk in and out of the cave.

"The white part of the map is where the cave continues, but is not suitable for public tours. It has been explored for over a half a mile beyond where we will go today. The areas in blue are where the cave tunnel is underwater. Divers have investigated these areas and found more passages beyond. At the very back, it gets too narrow to continue further. However, scientists put dye in the water and watched for where it would come out in the Burren. They found that some of the dye came out from a nearby hill, and some of it actually came out in Galway Bay."

As the tour began the walk through the cave, Molly tried to control her fear. After all, the last time she was in a cave, she and Paddy were almost roasted alive by a fire-breathing dragon.

"One of the interesting features about our cave is over here. Does anyone know what these are?" Molly saw only some shallow craters in the dirt. Everyone in the tour group was shaking their head no, while Shannon simply smiled and said nothing. "These are bear pits, hollowed out for when the bears hibernated." Amy explained. "We know these are bear pits, because we have bear skeletons right over here." She pushed a button, and light flooded a pile of white bones under the rock ledge. "These are brown bears. Brown bears have been extinct in Ireland for over 1,000 years. We have carbon dated these bones to about 1,200 years ago. Because bears used to live in the cave, we have adopted the brown bear as the symbol of Aillwee Cave, and use it on all of our signs."

Molly remembered how all of the signs that pointed the way to the cave had a silhouette of a bear on them. She had wondered what it meant.

"Ooh, wouldn't it be scary to be in a cave with bears?" whispered a girl standing behind Molly.

"I've seen worse," Molly muttered under her breath.

As they walked deeper into the cave, Amy pointed out various features like the stalactites that hung from the ceiling like a "bunch o' carrots," the straw stalactites that were thousands of years old, and the place where tall people were likely to bump their heads.

An iron bridge built to cross a deep chasm snaked through a very tall, deep part of the cave. A waterfall emerged high above them, tumbling noisily to the rocks below. "This is the Cascade Chamber," Amy announced. "Beyond this point we had to remove some boulders and enlarge the tunnel slightly. I'm sure you'll see why we thought it was important to extend the path deeper into the cave."

The group moved carefully through a very narrow passage, then through several large caverns. Some minutes later they arrived at the end of the path, in the middle of a very large space. Amy turned to talk to them again. "You can see where the cave continues on the other side. Much of it is underwater, and you can hear the sound of the river most of the time. This chamber is 90 meters by 20 meters, a very large space. We're going to turn out the lights for a few seconds so you can see how dark it is here. Please make sure you are holding the handrail firmly." She reached over to a panel and switched the lights out.

Molly did the math in her head. *About 270 feet long, 60 feet high. That's large enough for a couple of dragons.* Although the blackness engulfed her, she was fully expecting the dark to be split by the fire-spout of a black dragon with a blue racing stripe. She gripped the handrail fiercely.

More than one person sighed with relief as the lights came back on. Amy thanked the group, pointing them to the man-made tunnel that would lead them straight back to the entrance.

Shannon and Molly walked side-by-side down the exit tunnel. "Well, Molly, didja learn anyt'ing interestin', then?"

"Yes. It's cold inside a cave."

Shannon laughed merrily and hugged the little girl as they walked. "Let's see if we can get somet'in' to warm ya up at the café, then!"

That turned out to be a good plan, as it was still pouring outside when they entered the gift shop. They each ordered soup, Molly got the tomato soup while Shannon picked vegetable. They split a chicken wrap, and had some hot tea with brown bread and butter on the side.

"Mmm ... this is better." Molly slurped a spoonful of her warm, creamy soup.

"I toadly aghee," Shannon said with a mouthful of chicken wrap, making Molly giggle.

"Aunt Shannon, you made soup come out of my nose! Gross!"

"That's what napkins are for. Get used to laughing if ya stick around me." She pushed the napkin dispenser closer to Molly.

Several napkins and a delicious lunch later, they stepped outside to find the rain had vanished, leaving in its place a beautiful sunny afternoon. "That's Ireland for ya," Shannon sighed.

Walking back to the car, Molly noticed a set of large stone steps framed by a simple archway that led up the hillside about ten feet then disappeared from view as they turned to the left. A sign hung on the archway, engraved with the words "Mountain Walk."

"What's that, Aunt Shannon?"

"Let's investigate. Are ya wearing your boots?"

Climbing the steps, Molly discovered that at the top the steps blended into the now familiar rocks of the Burren. A rough path was visible leading up the hillside.

The climb was steep, but not unmanageable. Soon Molly and her aunt were forty feet above the welcome center. The view across the valley to the west was breathtaking. Lush green fields covered the far hillside, each divided by stone walls that crisscrossed the entire area.

"Look there, Molly!" Shannon was pointing to the north.

"Wow. That's Ballyvaughan way up there, right? And that's Galway Bay behind it?"

"Ya got it. The cave entrance is only halfway up this hill, and we still have an incredible view from here!" Shannon looked at her watch. "Oh, dear. I hate to cut our day short, but I do have to go to Doolin today. Let's stop in at the Farm House we passed on the way up, I can't leave without getting some of their fudge. And ya can see where they make all kinds of cheese."

"That sounds yummy. I'm glad we took the time to find out what the 'Mountain Walk' was. It's beautiful!"

chapter twelve

Second Wish

Molly waited only a few minutes after her aunt's car disappeared down the road before packing water and a snack into her backpack and racing up the green road to the Burren. Once she was away from the village, she began to stroke her silver bracelet. "Paddy, come and find me if it's safe."

She was not surprised when she reached the ringfort without seeing any sign of the leprechaun. Keeping a lookout for hikers, she scrambled over the broken wall. Stroking her bracelet again, she whispered "Is it safe enough here?"

"Safe enough, I reckon." Paddy peeked around a pile of the rubble and stood up. "How was th' cave?"

"I thought the dragon was going to pop up at any minute and toast everybody there. I don't think it's his cave, though. But it has plenty of rooms large enough to hold him."

"That's one surprise you and th' tourist industry can do without. I do have another surprise for ye, though."

"Really? What is it?"

"More of a 'who' is it, I'd say." The new voice came from atop the ringfort wall. Molly looked up to see a leprechaun sitting there cross-legged, smoking a clay pipe. His chin jutted out, made more defiant by the thick red beard. A worn top hat similar to Paddy's rested on his head.

Paddy grinned and began, "Molly O'Malley, this is me friend Kevin O'Brien. Kevin's agreed to..."

"I know who she is, Paddy! I've agreed to nuttin' but to see her for meself, and if possible, bring ye to your senses." Kevin uncrossed his legs and pointed at Molly with his pipe stem. "She's a big 'un! And ye know that big 'uns can't be trusted! One of these days she'll betray us all!"

"Man. Sounds like somebody got up on the wrong side of the bed this morning." Molly pulled her pack from her shoulders as she continued, "Nice to meet you, Kevin. You wouldn't believe how much you sound like Paddy did the day I met him."

Kevin stared, his face turning purple with rage. "I'll not be turnin' into a friend of the humans any time soon! My place is with the leprechauns, and you'll do well to remember that!"

"As is mine, Kevin," Paddy growled. "Don't accuse me of betrayin' th' leprechauns. I've risked a great deal for our folk, and for that matter, so has Molly here. A bit o' respect would be in order."

Kevin clamped his teeth on his pipe stem. "Very well, then. I understand that ye used a *wish*" — he glared at Paddy — "to find the thief and the gold. Not that we are any closer to punishin' the thief or recauverin' the gold."

"You make it sound as if we are responsible for the dragon," Molly responded. "Believe me; I'm just as scared of the dragon as you are."

Kevin nervously adjusted his jacket collar. "Who said I'm scared o' the dragon?"

"Molly's just saying that because she figured ye were an intelligent leprechaun, and anyone with any smarts is goin' to be careful around a fire-breathing dragon," Paddy smirked.

"Anyone with any smarts is goin' to be careful around humans, too," Kevin sputtered, his face scarlet. "I've wasted enough time here. If you want to ignore common sense, go ahead and talk to this— human, but mind me warning!" He rose and climbed down the far side of the wall.

"Well, that went well." Paddy gave a low whistle.

Molly sighed. "Do I have that effect on all leprechauns?"

"It's not you, girl, it's th' fact that you're human. It takes a while to figure out that you're not a typical human, as we describe 'em."

Molly rummaged around in her backpack. "I think it's more that you're not a typical leprechaun. Most of your people would have vanished the first chance they got instead of helping me out that day. Ah, here it is." She emerged holding a yellow apple. "I brought a golden delicious for you today." She tossed it to Paddy, who caught it with both hands.

"T'ank ye, Molly." He set the apple down. "I'm not a typical leprechaun?"

She took a bite out of her own apple. "Well, look at how Kevin reacted. He couldn't wait to get away from me. From what you've told me, that's pretty standard among leprechauns. All the stories are about how cruel and greedy people are. But you ... " she wiped juice from her chin, "hung around long enough to get to know me better, in spite of everything you had been taught. That's special. There's good people and bad people. You just took the time to sort out what kind of person I am."

Paddy eyed the girl intently. "You're forgettin' somet'ing. You have problems with your family. Your mother is ill, your father is gone most o' th' time, and you've been separated from both of them. Still, you've decided to help me and help th' leprechauns with *our* problem. You're th' special one."

Molly looked at the little man through the tears glistening in her eyes. "I know. I don't stop thinking about my family. Maybe we both just needed someone we could trust."

"Aye." Paddy picked up his apple and began to eat it. "That's not th' reason ye came up here, though. What's going on?"

She wiped her eyes and pushed her hair back. "The dragon, of course. What can we do to get rid of the dragon and get the gold back?"

"I've been givin' that some t'ought. We're not big enough to fight it physically. What about using poison to kill it? Then we wouldn't destroy th' cave, and could still get th' gold out afterward."

"Yuck." Molly made a face. "Paddy, I couldn't stand the thought of poisoning any living creature. Besides, we don't even know what it eats. What would we put the poison on?"

Paddy sighed. "I'm runnin' out o' ideas."

"Well, we can't talk to it. The last time we were even close to it, we almost got barbequed." Molly frowned. "Let's just try to keep thinking of things we can do."

Two days later Molly hiked up into the Burren, stroking her silver bracelet. "Paddy, come out, come out, wherever you are," she hummed to herself.

A subdued pop sounded beside her. "Hi, Paddy. This bracelet is really coming in handy."

"Aye," the leprechaun replied. "Now we can be stumped as to what to do next more quickly than ever."

"Maybe not," Molly said dreamily. "I think I know what we have to do."

"*Have* to do? I don't like th' sound o' that, Molly. Are ye plannin' what I t'ink you're plannin'?"

"Probably. Paddy, we've tried everything that we can to figure out what to do about that dragon. We can't go to the grownups, because we can't let them know about the fairy world. They wouldn't believe me anyway. We can't go to the fairies, they've helped us out enough already, and as you said earlier, this is a leprechaun problem."

"So you've decided, then?"

Molly folded her arms. "It's time to use the second wish."

Paddy sighed. "It's th' most powerful t'ing we have. I just hope we can use it properly. Let's talk about how we phrase it, then."

Nodding, Molly sat down on a rock. "If we get too specific, it might not solve the problem. For example, if we asked for a machine gun, we might get one without any bullets. Not that either of us know how to use a machine gun anyway."

"I might be able to dig up a troll who could manage," Paddy offered.

"Paddy, I'm being serious here!" Molly scolded. "I think we need to be specific as to solving the problem, without being specific as to *how* to solve the problem. You cast a marvelous wish spell, we need to use the power that's in it."

"I t'ink you're right, girl. Do ye have any ideas about th' phrasing, then?"

"We already have some information from the first wish. I think we should use that. We know that it is a dragon that is stealing the leprechaun's gold."

"Agreed. What else can ye say to make it more specific?"

"Well, that's just it. If we make the request for the solution too specific, like asking for a particular type of weapon, that could be a mistake. We don't know what will work against a black dragon."

"Hmmm ... Then should ye make th' wish more general instead?"

Molly nodded. "I think that's the best way. I have to say something about being granted the solution to the specific problem."

Paddy exhaled. "Right, then. Are we ready?"

"Yes. Where do we want to do this?"

"Let's go into that stand o' trees just below th' hill. That will give us some privacy."

They climbed down to the grove, finding that the trees enclosed a small clearing. "This should be good," Paddy said as he looked around.

Molly opened her locket. Her parents' pictures looked as happy as ever, even as she recalled that none of them were too happy in real life right now. If only she could wish the problems with her family away. She removed the shamrock from inside the locket and held it in her hand. She closed the locket with a snap.

One problem at a time, she thought. There's still another wish left after this one. "Here goes, then. I wish that we would be granted the solution to the problem of the dragon that is stealing from the leprechauns."

Again the shamrock glowed with a brilliant green light. The light formed into a ball as it did before, and floated about 50 feet away from Molly and Paddy into the clearing.

Molly replaced the shamrock in her locket and looked at the ball of light. "Do we follow it again?" she asked.

Abruptly the light exploded with a flash and was gone. In its place sat a creature about 30 feet long, with large, bat-like wings, and glittering white scales that covered it from the tip of its nose to the end of its long, serpentine tail. Horns curved backward from its head almost to its long, supple neck. The creature blinked its violet eyes and looked around.

Paddy exhaled softly. "Great. Just what we needed. Another dragon."

chapter thirteen

Stanley

Paddy nudged Molly gently and whispered, "Very slowly, start moving to your left, so as not to alarm it. We need to get behind those trees."

Molly nodded and whispered. "Okay."

As she began to move, the dragon's eyes immediately turned to follow her. Its head tilted, as if curious. "Excuse me," it said. "I wonder if you can help me understand what's going on."

Molly and Paddy froze. They looked at each other, then back to the glittering white dragon.

"Did he..." asked Molly.

"Yes, he did." replied Paddy.

"Did I what?" asked the dragon.

"Um... you talked," said Molly.

"Well, of course," said the dragon. He stretched and let his wings unfold for a moment, then tucked them back against his sides. "You can talk, can't you?"

"Well, yes, we can talk," Paddy agreed. "But we're not dragons. If that's what ye are."

The dragon looked at them strangely. "Yes, I'm a dragon. Do you know other dragons that can't talk?"

"We're not sure," Molly offered. "This is all very confusing."

The dragon looked up at the sky, then at the hills surrounding the meadow. "Oh, my," he said. "Can I ask you something?"

"Go ahead," said Paddy, "I suppose so."

"We're... not in Ellesyndria, are we?"

"Where?" asked Molly.

The dragon sighed. "I was afraid of that. That was an awfully strange feeling that accompanied that green light. It just smelled of magic. Can you tell me where I am, then?"

Molly and Paddy looked at each other, and then looked back at the dragon. "You're in Ireland," Molly began.

"Ireland." The dragon mused. "You mean, on Earth."

"Well, yes," said Molly, "where else would you be?"

"As I said, in Ellesyndria."

Molly blurted out the question that had been on her mind for a few minutes. "Are you going to eat us?"

The dragon blinked his bright violet eyes. "Eat you? I should think not. If I ate you, I wouldn't get any of my questions answered, would I?"

"No, I suppose not," said Molly. "You have questions?"

"Of course I have questions," said the dragon. "But I think we had better start with introductions and go from there."

The dragon examined the grass beneath him and picked a comfortable spot in which to sit down. "My name is Stanley. I have been living in Ellesyndria for many years now. Speaking of years, what year is it here?"

"It's 2007," replied Molly.

"2007?" the dragon murmured. "Well that matches up, at least. Time must continue at the same rate in both places."

"Excuse me, but what is this 'Ellesyndria' ye keep talkin' about?" asked Paddy.

Stanley turned to him with a smile that crinkled the corners of his mouth. "I was born just across the Irish Sea in England, years ago. Eventually I was able to escape to Ellesyndria, a— how should I put this?— a haven to protect the dragons. It appears that you have summoned me back to Earth. I just hope that you have a *really* good reason."

"I'm Paddy Finegan," announced the leprechaun. "I'm not sure what you're doing here, either."

Molly looked at Paddy. "Do you remember when the green light went down into the pothole? And we decided to trust it, even though we didn't know what was going on?" She gulped and looked up at the white dragon, who was staring at her with great interest. "I think we're going to have to trust it again."

She walked up to the great dragon. "My name is Molly O'Malley. We're trying to find the solution to a problem that the leprechauns have."

Stanley raised an eyebrow. "Leprechauns? So they *do* exist." He nodded at Paddy. "And what problem would that be?"

"Something is stealing their gold. We couldn't figure out what it was, so Paddy cast a spell to grant me three wishes."

The dragon lay down in front of her, crossing his front paws. "Oh, this is getting interesting. Please continue."

"For my first wish, I asked to find who or what was stealing the gold. A strange green light led us to an underground cavern, where we found a black, fire-breathing dragon."

"A dragon? Here?" said Stanley, raising his large ears in surprise.

"Is it a dragon ye weren't expecting, or the fact that he's here?" Paddy questioned.

"We'll get to that in time. Please go on."

"We couldn't figure out what to do about it, since the dragon is large and obviously very dangerous," Molly continued. "So I used the second wish just now to summon a solution to the problem. And *you* appeared."

"Really?" said Stanley. "That is *very* interesting."

"Well," Paddy said, "we've told ye our side of it. Maybe if you told us some more about yourself, we could start puttin' some more pieces o' this puzzle together."

"Very well," said Stanley. "Where should I start? I was born in the year 1157 and lived in England with my Uncle Alfonso. I grew up during the time of knights, kings and castles. Is that still going on?"

"Not so much," Molly replied. "That all ended some time ago. The world is much different now."

Stanley shook his head. "Changed for the better, I hope. Humans had started to develop weapons that endangered the dragons. They began to hunt and kill us wherever we were found."

"That's awful," Molly said sadly. "What did you do?"

"We tried to fight back at first, but there were too many men. Many of our friends fell to the hunters. Then one day, just as things looked darkest, the great friend of the dragons appeared."

"Who's that?" Molly asked.

"Morubek. He was a powerful wizard who took pity on the plight of the dragons. He could not stand to see such magnificent creatures destroyed." He stretched out an arm luxuriously, extending the sharp talons at the end of his foot. Molly gulped again.

Stanley smiled. "What Morubek did was to cast the most powerful spell he had ever summoned. He opened the Arch of Rima."

"The Arch of... Rima? What's that?" Molly asked.

"It was a gateway to another world. A gateway to the world of Ellesyndria. Ellesyndria is a world of lush grass, trees and flowers, beautiful mountains and streams, and most importantly, nothing that would cause harm to dragonkind. It's a world where dragons live in peace, and are not hunted by men. Morubek opened the gateway at the appointed time, and all of the dragons that had gathered together flew through the arch to safety. The Arch then closed behind us forever."

"What year was this?" asked Paddy.

"It was the year 1317," Stanley replied.

"Aye," Paddy said, his eyes focused far away. "And there have been no reported sightings o' dragons since that time. Until now, anyway. So *that's* what happened."

"Then you're almost a thousand years old?" asked Molly.

"Closer to 850," Stanley said modestly. "Dragons live a very long time. I was only about 160 when we went through the Arch."

"How did ye manage to get all o' th' dragons together at one time?" Paddy asked.

"Dragon messengers were sent all over Europe. It was Morubek's idea. They passed the message that there was a way to escape all of the terrible things that were going on. I remember that circumstances were grim for everyone. For three years before we left, it rained nearly all the time. Crops would spoil because they couldn't dry out. Men couldn't feed their own animals because the hay rotted in the field. Many people started going hungry. Maybe that's why men were hunting us."

"Maybe they t'ought you were causin' it," grumbled Paddy. "Men always blame th' t'ings they don't understand on someone else."

"That's a possibility," said Stanley. "So what's this problem that you're having?"

"I guess it's my turn," sighed Paddy. "Several years ago some o' th' leprechauns started havin' their gold stolen." He looked up at the dragon. "Ye know about leprechauns, then?"

Stanley nodded. "Yes, I've heard of you. I had a friend in England who told me stories about the little people. He was a knight who traveled all over. He told my Uncle and me much about the world of humans as well. I wasn't sure whether to believe him or not, but here you are."

"We didn't know what it was that was takin' our gold. There were no clues that could tell us who or what th' thief was. Not until I met Molly a few weeks ago."

Stanley turned his gaze to Molly. "What's your place in all of this, then?" he said gently.

"I just came to Ireland to stay with my aunt for a few weeks or longer. I was lonely, and mad because I didn't want to come, so I hiked up into the Burren one day and met Paddy. We talked and became friends. After a while we both got the same idea of using the wishes to help the leprechauns. He had to use the spell on me, because he couldn't give the wishes to himself or to another leprechaun."

"Very noble," said Stanley. "He must place a lot of faith in you."

"How can you sit there and talk to me like that, when people like me were hunting the dragons to extinction?" asked Molly, trembling.

"Oh, I don't think those people were very much like you. I've met a few humans that I felt I could trust. From what I've heard about leprechauns... " he winked a large violet eye at Paddy... "If Paddy trusts you, I feel pretty safe trusting you, too."

"Aye," said Paddy, "ye can find a wee bit o' good in humans, if ye meet the right ones." The trio looked at each other as the sound of birds echoed from the trees.

Paddy spoke first. "The next t'ing to do is to decide what to do with you, Stanley. People in the modern world aren't goin' to be accustomed to seeing a dragon walking about."

"Is it worse than when I left?" Stanley asked.

Molly nodded. "You would not believe the weapons that men have now. Bows and arrows are considered worthless today."

"Okay, then. Any suggestions?" said Stanley.

"Th' woods are not too bad a place, except when people come through them. There are hikers that pass through fairly frequently." Paddy looked around to make sure they were not being watched. "Th' Burren itself has some rocks that could provide cover, but nuttin' large enough to hide you. One o' th' cathairs might be tall enough, but hikers walk up to look at them as well."

"But this other dragon stays hidden underground, you say?"

Molly gave a little squeal. "That's right! The Burren has lots of caves and underground rivers. But the pothole we found is much too small for you to fit through."

"And much too small for the black dragon as well, wouldn't you say?" Stanley winked.

"That means," Molly murmured, "there must be another way to get into the cave, someplace big enough for the dragon to get in! If you can find the way in, you could hide underground too!"

"Underground rivers, did you say?" asked Stanley.

"Yes," said Molly. "My aunt took me to Aillwee Cave. Divers explored some of the flooded tunnels where the river was. Even though they couldn't follow them all the way, they put dye in the water so they could tell where the water ran out. They found that it ran out into Galway Bay!" She pointed in the direction of the water. "So it is possible that the dragon's cave has an exit to the bay, although it could be underwater."

Stanley shrugged. "It shouldn't be too much of a problem. Dragons actually live in the water for the first ten or so years of their life. I was in a lake where we lived. We're very good swimmers, although you may not think so to look at us."

Paddy jumped up. "Yes, that could explain how th' dragon could get in and out o' th' cave without bein' seen! He'd just swim through th' underwater tunnel into th' Bay, and come up along th' shoreline where no people would see him."

"When it gets dark, then, you should show me this pothole, and we can search along the shoreline in the bay for an opening." Stanley grunted with satisfaction.

"Howareya goin' to find an underwater opening in th' dark, now?" demanded Paddy.

"Didn't you mention that this dragon was sitting on a large pile of gold?" Stanley asked quietly.

Paddy's eyes opened wide with understanding. "Are ye tellin' me ye can just smell th' gold, and it'll take ye right to it?"

"Something like that. Dragons are very attuned to finding gold." He grinned at Paddy's visible outrage. "Don't worry, Paddy. I overcame my lust for gold many centuries ago. Not an easy thing for a dragon to do, either, let me tell you. I'll help you get the gold back for the leprechauns. It doesn't look like I'll be doing anything else for a while."

"And just how do ye expect to get th' gold away from a fire breathin' dragon? You'll likely burn down everyt'ing in County Clare if ye two get to fightin'!"

Stanley smiled as if he was about to hand out birthday presents. "Oh, that's right, I haven't told you yet, have I?" He puckered his lips and blew lightly. A cloud of white sparkled in the afternoon sun, spinning down in showers of delicate snowflakes to coat Molly and Paddy's hair and shoulders. Paddy looked at the white stuff in astonishment, while Molly felt a slight shiver.

The white dragon winked. "I don't breathe fire. I breathe ice."

chapter fourteen

Fire and Ice

It was decided that Molly would return to her house while Paddy and Stanley searched for the underwater opening. "I'll find you later," Molly called over her shoulder, tapping the silver bracelet. "I can't risk getting grounded again."

Paddy and Stanley made themselves as invisible as possible in the woods. This proved to be very difficult for Stanley. "It's not workin', Stan, you're just not blendin' in."

Stanley turned a baleful eye on the leprechaun. "Well, Paddy, I've always leaned more toward the unique than toward the blending in type. Unless you want me to cough up several feet of snow drifts to hide in."

Paddy grinned. "No, I don't t'ink so. Snow drifts in Eire would likely attract as much attention as a dragon. We'll have to t'ink o' somet'in' else."

"Can you cast a camouflage spell? Something that would make me look like an object with the same basic size and shape, just for a few hours?"

"What didja have in mind?"

"How about a white boulder?"

Paddy thought about it. "Hide ye right out in th' open, eh? Not a bad idea. There's a good outcropping over here. Th' Burren rocks are generally flat and low. I'd recommend that ye flatten out as much as possible instead o' curlin' up in a ball."

"Good. Then we can talk about what we need to do after dark."

Stanley stretched out between some existing rocks. Paddy gathered some hazel that was plentiful and stacked it next to the dragon. "This stuff hides most o' th' stone walls along the roadways. It ought to do a fair job o' hidin' you." He muttered some words and Stanley's form melted into the surrounding rock field and hazel scrub brush, as far as anyone but Paddy could see.

Paddy found a place near Stanley's head, hidden from any passersby. "Grand! Now we can talk. First t'ing: I'll take ye to th' pothole, so you'll know where th' black dragon is. Maybe that will help us find where th' entrance to th' cave might be."

"I agree. Let's assume that I find the cave entrance, and I can get into the cave itself. What's our plan?"

Paddy scratched his head. "To tell ye th' truth, I don't know. It's only been a couple o' hours that we've had a white dragon to work with."

"Hmmm ... Okay, how about this? I'll try to draw the black dragon out of the cave. It might not be too hard if he thinks he's threatened. The tight quarters of the cave would make it too difficult for real fighting, and fire-breathers tend to use up all of the breathable air when they're blasting in enclosed places."

"How do ye know all o' that?" Patty was skeptical.

"My Uncle Alfonso is a fire-breather. Believe me, I have hundreds of years of experience in what fire-breathers can do."

"Alright, I'll take your word for it. What happens after ye get him out o' th' cave?"

"We can't fight underwater; we'll both have to come up for air. I'll try to lead him up here. The hills are pretty high in this part of the Burren, and they form a natural bowl in the middle. The black dragon is going to try to fly to get an advantage with his fire-breath, and I'm going to need room to maneuver, too. This gives us our best shot at having enough air space to fly, but still hide what is going on from anyone outside the bowl. The hills that form the sides of the bowl will hide us, if we can keep from flying too high."

"*You* know that, but what's to keep th' black dragon from flyin' higher and bein' seen?" Paddy growled.

Stanley smiled. "I think our friend the black dragon is an expert at hiding, himself. Didn't it take a wish for the leprechauns to even find out that he existed?"

"Right..."

"I think we have to count on the black dragon's sense of self-preservation to stay low enough even while flying to avoid giving himself away. It's going to be tricky, with flames shooting off in the middle of the night."

"What then?"

Stanley sighed. "My best advantage is that the black dragon may not know much about other dragons, and hopefully nothing at all about an ice-breathing dragon. I don't know how long this dragon was here before the rest of us escaped to Ellesyndria. Perhaps a mix of surprise and the unknown factor of my ice-breath will let me subdue the dragon."

"Subdue it? I t'ought ye were goin' to kill it!"

Stanley was silent for a moment. When he spoke again, his voice was quiet. "Paddy, I have encountered many things in my life that I didn't understand. If I had killed each of those things, I would have missed out on a lot. I would have destroyed people who became dear friends. I would have killed people who later helped me and helped others. I was very fortunate to have learned at an early age to try to understand first, rather than conquer. What would have happened if I had attacked a strange girl and a leprechaun earlier today?"

Now Paddy was silent. "I see your point," he muttered at last. "I never really saw th' black dragon as somet'in' to be understood. It stole our gold, it was a threat. Not an individual. Not somet'in' with feelings."

"Oh, dragons have feelings. We have to act with the belief that we can reach those feelings. Perhaps I can subdue the dragon, and force him to listen to reason. But I would rather reason with him if at all possible. He is my kindred."

"But th' wish summoned ye to solve th' problem o' th' black dragon, and th' theft o' th' gold!"

"Did the wish dictate how the problem would be solved?"

Paddy hung his head. "O' course not."

"Trust my instincts on this, Paddy. A wish is a powerful thing. There has to be something else at work here. Let's wait for nightfall."

Some hours later, the sky began to dim. Paddy had left some time earlier, but Stanley remained still to preserve the camouflage spell. Now he raised his head to look around, and the enchanted hazel fell off all around him.

"Paddy?" The violet eyes searched the dusk, and the white ears perked up. "Oh, no ... "

The white dragon crept toward the nearby grove, keeping low to the ground with his wings folded tightly to his side. He shook his head in disappointment as he entered the clearing.

Paddy Finegan was propped up against a tree, a pewter mug in his right hand, and a half-empty bottle in his left. The leprechaun was singing in the twilight:

Me life was so certain,
me pleasures were grand,
me work was exquisite
ye should understand.

Then came th' great terror
that took all th' gold,
in secret, in darkness
with thefts all so bold.

But came a rare moment,
a girl with red hair,
who captured me poor heart
With loving and care.

I granted her wishes,
all three for a friend,
to stop th' great terror,
th' darkness to end.

But now th' great savior
a dragon o' ice,
says: to this great terror
we all must be NICE!

Paddy shouted the final word and took another swig from his mug. Stanley walked up to him and sniffed the bottle.

"Whiskey?" he asked the leprechaun softly.

Paddy looked up at him with blood-shot eyes. "Th' finest Irish whiskey. Would ye like some?"

Stanley shook his head sadly and lay down beside the drunken leprechaun. "Paddy, would you do something for me?"

Paddy turned his face up to the large white head. "Anythin', me friend."

"I'd like you to stay here until Molly comes back. But you have to be very, very quiet and not let anyone see you. Do you understand?"

Paddy held a finger up to his lips. "Quiet as th' grave. I'll be invisi... inbisivile... no one will see me."

"Good man," Stanley whispered. "Tell Molly I'll be back as soon as I can. One more thing, can you point me in the general direction of the pothole where the black dragon is?"

Paddy pointed out a direction. "It's about halfway up a hill, about two kilometers, maybe."

"Kilometers?"

Paddy looked at the dragon. "Oh, that's right, you're an Englishhh dragon. Just a little over a mile."

Stanley smiled. "Thank you, Paddy. Now remember ..."

"Quiet. Wait for Molly." Paddy raised his mug.

The white dragon unfolded his wings, and leaping into the air, gathered speed as he glided low over the Burren hillside.

Molly approached the grove cautiously, using her flashlight as little as possible. When she reached the clearing she stroked her bracelet and whispered, "Paddy! I'm here!"

The clearing appeared deserted. She was not worried as she knew the dragon and the leprechaun planned to hide when she left. She tapped her bracelet this time. "Paddy! Where are you?"

Hic!

Molly looked up into the tree where the sound came from. On a branch fifteen feet up, Paddy dangled his feet and covered his mouth with an empty bottle. "'Scuse me," he said, and laughed.

"What are you doing? Come down here at once!"

Paddy descended a bit shakily and collapsed on the ground at her feet. "I'm glad ye came back, Molly, I've been waiting for ye."

"That's not all you've been doing. Where is Stanley?"

"Oh, he went off to find th' pothole and th' dragon." His eyes welled up with tears. "Didja know that we're not goin' to kill th' dragon? We're goin' to make him our friend." He tipped his mug up for another drink, looking confused when he found it empty. "And after we make him our friend, he's goin' to barbeque us."

"Paddy, are you *drunk?* How could you do this tonight of all nights? Why aren't you helping Stanley?"

"Don't be too hard on him, Molly. He doesn't understand yet."

Molly whirled to find the white dragon behind her, dripping wet. He smelled faintly of sea-salt.

"Stanley, what's going on?"

"First off, I found the entrance to the cave. It's just as you suspected; an underwater entrance large enough to let a dragon through. It's a tight squeeze, but I could manage."

"Did he see ye, then?" Paddy's eyes were wide.

"No. I came back to let you know what was happening so you could find cover. There will probably be some serious action after I lead him up to the bowl between the hills."

"Thanks, Stanley. At least someone was doing something productive tonight." Molly glared at Paddy, who looked positively miserable. "What did Paddy mean when he said we were going to make friends with the black dragon?"

Stanley looked sadly at the unhappy leprechaun. "I plan to try and get the black dragon to talk to us. Paddy was counting on me killing the black dragon to get the gold back. I can't do that to a fellow dragon, not unless it's self defense. We'll have to see if the black dragon tries to kill me." He smiled with an effort. "That's a distinct possibility, with all the taunting I'm going to give him."

Molly hoisted Paddy up by an elbow. "Come on, Mr. Finegan, we need to find someplace safe. Let's go up between the hills and find some nice big rocks to hide behind."

"Are ye mad at me, Molly? I didn't mean anythin' by it, I was just thinkin' about gettin' rid o' th' black dragon, and now we're goin' to make friends with th' beast, and it was getting' so confusin' ... "

The young girl dropped his elbow and spun to face him. "You don't think that things are confusing for anyone else? Do you think I know what's going to happen next with the dragon? I don't even know what's going to happen next with my mom and dad! But that doesn't give me an excuse to get drunk! How does that solve anything? How does that even help you think clearly? You can barely stand on your own!"

Paddy nodded vacantly. "It's a fine mess I've made o' things, that's for sure. But th' dragon... "

"Is out of our hands now. Stanley has a plan, he's the one the second wish brought to us, and we have to believe in the power of the wish!"

Paddy gave a low cry. "But I didn't believe! I don't know what happened to me that night that I gave ye th' wishes! I wanted so bad for th' wishes to be real for ye. I don't know how it happened, but... "

"Paddy. Look at Stanley." Shaking, he turned to take in the great white dragon, his scales glistening with the sea water. "Stanley is *real*. The wishes are *real*. We are not playing make-believe, and I need you to be here with me instead of emptying a bottle of whatever you were drinking! Can you do that, Paddy?"

"Aye. I'll do it for ye, girl. If you believe in th' wishes, then I believe in ye."

Molly sighed. "Then that will do for now. I hope leprechauns sober up fast." She looked at Stanley. "You be careful. It sounds to me like you're putting yourself in danger tonight. If it gets too difficult, take care of yourself first. I don't want you to get hurt on my account or Paddy's."

Stanley lowered his head to her level. His huge violet eyes shone in the nearly full moon. "I don't know what's going to happen next either, dear girl. I can only promise that I will try to be as brave as you."

Molly's eyes filled with tears. "I don't know how much longer I can be brave."

"I have to agree with Paddy. I believe in *you*." He smiled. "Find your cover quickly. I'll be back in ten minutes. Hopefully, with company." Launching himself into the air, he vanished into the darkness.

"C'mon, Paddy," Molly muttered as she blinked back her tears. "We need to go." She paused, remembering that her father used the same words when he picked her up at school. It seemed like that was ages ago. She tugged Paddy to his feet and they stumbled up the hill together.

"Over here." Molly pulled the compliant elf behind a raised rock shelf. She could almost carry him under her arm, she thought. A smile creased her face, maybe she would tell him that later after he sobered up.

From their vantage point, they had a reasonably good view of the bowl between the hills. The moon was only a few days past full, and its pale light reflected off the light colored limestone that paved the ground.

A sound rumbled through the night, brief but throaty. Molly thought it sounded like something she had heard once before, what was it? Oh, yes, a hot air balloon...

Looking like a ghost in the moonlight, Stanley lifted silently over the ridge and descended into the valley. His wings pivoted as he slowed to catch the breeze, and then he thrust himself into a tight turn.

Rocketing over the ridge behind him, flying a little higher, the black dragon fell out of the sky like a cannonball in slow motion. He stretched out his wings to gain altitude briefly as the dragons approached each other in the center of the natural arena.

Flames roared from the black dragon's mouth, white-hot with blue and yellow flowing around the center stream. "That's what sounds like a hot air balloon," Molly whispered.

At the same instant, a cone of frost spiraled from Stanley's mouth, the ice crystals sparkling unnaturally in the night.

The two streams collided with a hiss, ice crystals reflecting firelight in all directions before they melted into clouds of steam. The fire paused in its course, dimming quickly from the blue and white to a gentle golden glow as it went out.

Spots swam before Molly's eyes as she struggled to regain her night vision. The dragons swept by each other at a frighteningly close distance, the black snapping in frustration at Stanley as he passed. Each made a slow, sweeping turn, flapping their wings to gain altitude, and came at each other again.

This time the black dragon spat small bursts of fire at Stanley, weaving back and forth so that the fireballs converged from different angles. Stanley dodged several of them with a magnificent twist in midair, and picked off the last three with ice-balls of his own.

Once more the dragons turned, keeping low over the depression between the hills.

"Stanley was right," Paddy murmured groggily as they watched. "Th' other dragon *is* stayin' low."

It seemed as if the two were going to hit each other this time. At the last moment the black dragon turned his head to the side as he veered past Stanley, shooting a long, continuous flame. It seared Stanley on his flank, even as he responded with a blast of his own that caught the black dragon squarely in the wing, pushing the fire breather into an uncontrolled roll. His flame missed Stanley widely, striking the rocks in front of where Molly and Paddy were hidden. Molly screamed and ducked below the rock edge, pulling Paddy down with her as the fire singed the hazel around them.

With amazing agility the black dragon pulled out of the roll and plummeted toward Molly. He pulled up sharply, blasting a bright ribbon of heat and light above their heads. Molly screamed again. Instead of attacking, the black dragon lit gently on the ground. Stanley raced to place his body between the fire breather and the two friends, his talons gripping the limestone as he skidded to a halt.

The dragons regarded each other quietly for a moment, each sucking in the night air after their exertions. Stanley spoke in a tongue strange to Molly's ears. The black dragon responded in kind, a silky, smooth string of sounds that was oddly soothing. Once more they exchanged phrases in the strange language, and Stanley turned to Molly.

"*Her* name is Nefra. She has agreed not to fight with us because... "

A voice issued from the black dragon, burning the words into Molly's brain. *"I will not fight with you for her sake."* Nefra's yellow eyes focused directly on Molly. The red-haired girl sat shaking behind the rock, holding in her arms a leprechaun who was now fully sober.

chapter fifteen

Nefra

"W-Why me? What do I have to do with this?" Molly stammered.

"I wish you no harm."

"Good," Stanley began. "We don't mean to harm you."

"Don't mean to harm me? You're tracking me, entering my home, breathing ice at me, and you mean me no harm?" Nefra's voice echoed inside Molly's head, as though she was thinking it instead of hearing it.

"We only want to talk."

"I will do it for her sake."

Molly sat on the ground, stunned.

Paddy pushed out of Molly's embrace and jumped up on the rock ledge. "And will ye give back th' gold ye took for her sake as well, then?"

Nefra stared at Paddy until he looked away. "Patience. We have much to discuss."

Paddy looked ready to protest again when Stanley cut him off. "I think that since we are talking now instead of holding a barbeque, we can take things a little slower. Wouldn't you agree, Paddy?"

Paddy jammed his hands into his pockets and glared up at Stanley. "For now, then. But just ye remember why we're here in th' first place!"

Stanley addressed Nefra again. "This is Paddy, and the girl is Molly."

Molly found her voice. "How did you come to be here? Why aren't you with the other dragons?"

Nefra turned her sleek head toward Molly. "You mean in Ellesyndria? I wasn't hatched yet."

Stanley staggered and sat down. "You know of Ellesyndria? How can that be, if you were not hatched?"

"I avoid men at all costs. It was not always so. In the beginning there was one. One who hatched me from my egg, and raised me until he died. He saved my life, and taught me who I was."

"A man who knew of dragons and of Ellesyndria? It's not possible! That was a great secret... "

"Not to the one, especially not to the one. I knew him as Father, but you may have known him as Morubek."

Stanley exhaled a chilling frost from his mouth that wilted the nearby heather. "Morubek. I was nearly the last to fly through the Arch, and his image is my final memory looking back through the gateway as it dissolved. He was standing there, waving. And he was crying; the greatest wizard of all time, with tears streaming down his wrinkled cheeks. He loved the dragons, and we left him alone."

Nefra lay down and shifted to find a comfortable spot. "Not all of the dragons flew through the Arch. My mother was brought down by the archers a mile short of the meeting place. Sh-she was carrying my egg with her." Her voice cracked as she finished.

"What happened to your father? Your mother's mate?"

"He died protecting her as they flew to the meeting place. His body was found a half mile from where she fell."

"I'm sorry, Nefra." Stanley lowered his head. "There were many dragons killed during that time. I lost a good friend myself." He smiled at the black dragon.

"The knights celebrated their victory afterward. They were so loud that they attracted the attention of Morubek, who was a short distance away. When he arrived, his rage could not be controlled."

"What happened?" Molly asked.

"He never told me. Morubek was a master of fire, and if his acts were as strong as his shame was afterward, I suspect the humans could have been later mistaken for victims of dragon-fire."

"But he found your egg." Stanley spoke softly.

"*Yes.*" Nefra lowered her head to the stone. A soft clink sounded, and Molly noticed something around the black dragon's neck.

"What's that you're wearing, Nefra?"

Nefra raised her head slightly so that her neck could be seen. "It is a gift — from a friend." Barely visible in the moonlight, a stone disc hung from a dark band of cloth.

"May I see it?"

"By all means." The dragon seemed very pleased.

Molly walked carefully over to the dragon, stepping carefully over the broken rock field. Leaning down, she switched her flashlight on to see the medallion.

The pattern was carved with several levels of depth. Molly thought the center looked like an eye, with a pupil like a cat's, thin and vertical. Around that was a raised circle with a bump in one spot. When she looked at the bump closer, it appeared to be a snake's head, and it was devouring the rest of its body. A large triangle surrounded the eye and the snake, and the whole was set in a circle with a strong, thick raised edge. The triangle and most of the eye were highly polished and flat, while the snake, the pupil, and the outside edge were rounded and stood higher than the polished part. The remainder was rough and cut deeper than the rest of the design.

Turning it over, Molly saw that the back was flat and unadorned. A hole sat just above the triangle and a brass ring set through it, so that the medallion could be hung. The medallion was suspended from Nefra's neck by a thin strip of cloth that appeared to be woven. Though blackened with age and beginning to wear along the sides, the cloth did not seem to be in danger of falling apart.

"This is really cool!"

"I'm glad that you like it, Molly."

"Nefra," said Stanley, "what happened after Morubek found your egg?"

"He kept my egg warm and safe until I hatched. Somehow he knew the dragon language, he was very proud of that. He taught me years, and told me that I was born in 1317."

"Just after the escape. What a shame — you were so close."

"Morubek cared for me, fed me. He named me. He said I was named after an ancient Egyptian queen who was very beautiful. I couldn't pronounce the name he told me, so he shortened it to Nefra."

"Nefertiri, I think," Molly said. "You speak very well now."

"It's been a long time. He taught me how to speak the old Irish tongue, so I could understand the language of men who might hunt me. But he also warned me to stay away from men, and remain hidden whenever possible.

"We lived by an inland lake for several years— I pretty much lived in it. There was very little food, for there was a great famine in the land. Father— Morubek had very little to eat. I became quite good at catching fish, and would share them with him. He survived for a while, but he became sick and died while I was still very young."

"So Morubek spent the rest of his life caring for dragons. It's what he would have wanted to do. I wish he would have had more time to be with you." Stanley sighed. "I know he was happy to help you, Nefra, even though he couldn't open the Arch again."

"I wish he would have had more time, too. He did tell me of my parents: my father, a pure black dragon, and my mother, who was a blue. He didn't know their names." She indicated the blue stripe that ran the length of her sinuous body. "I got the blue from my mother. The black has come in very handy over the years. I have been hiding since I was born."

She shivered as she continued her story. "When I was 31 years old, an evil thing came to Eire. Men huddled around campfires and whispered of something called the Black Death. I was lonely for the man, and crept in close to the camp to listen to them. But they saw me, and assumed that it was I that caused this disease. I fled, barely escaping their spears and arrows. From then on I only came out at night or in fog. Many men died from this Black Death, more than had died from the great famine thirty years before.

"I searched for years for a safe place to live and hide. There was a great cave in the high cliffs to the south of here. I could hide from those on the land there, but it was open to the sea, and I had to be careful not to be seen as I came and went. When more men came to the cliffs to marvel at their beauty, I decided to leave.

"I could fly at night— the fog is too dangerous for flying, even I can't see where to land— and I did a lot of swimming. I have been up and down the west coast of Eire, exploring cliffs and caves everywhere I could find them.

"Recently I returned to this area and swam up the coast, looking for shelter. This time I found the underwater entrance to my cave. It was perfect, until now." She glared at Stanley.

"What about th' gold? You've stolen gold from th' leprechauns! What haveyeh to say about that, then?" Paddy demanded.

Nefra looked at the defiant elf curiously. "Is that what you are, a leprechaun? I thought you were just little men. I have no love for men, for they killed my parents and hunted me. You little men are very good at acquiring gold. It is pleasant for me to lie on gold; it doesn't corrode or wear away, even the stone in my cave cracks and crumbles over time."

"She has a point, there," Stanley agreed. "A dragon's skin is naturally acidic. Gold is an ideal bedding material."

"Whose side are ye on?" Paddy yelled at Stanley, stomping his foot in rage.

"It became a game for me, to take the gold from the little men. I found that I could sense the gold, and when I located where it was hidden, I took it when the little men weren't there."

"How did ye carry it?"

"In Morubek's leather traveling cloak. I couldn't bear to part with it after he left. It's come in quite handy for hauling things I can't hold easily in my claws."

"Well, th' gold doesn't belong to men, it belongs to leprechauns, and we have as much trouble with men as dragons do!" Paddy bellowed.

Nefra regarded Paddy for a moment. "So Molly is a leprechaun, too?"

Paddy reddened as he looked over at Molly. "No, she's not a leprechaun, she's human — but she's special!"

"Yes, she is, isn't she?" Nefra purred.

Stanley jumped into the conversation. "This is all very interesting, but we have to take care of some things right away. Now, the first thing is how Nefra and I can keep from getting discovered. I'm sure that little fireworks display we put on was seen from somewhere. Even though no one is likely to come out to the Burren in the middle of the night ... "

"Ahem!" coughed Molly.

"... someone is bound to check it out tomorrow. The cave will work for now, but two dragons are harder to hide than one."

"Especially when th' newest arrival is sportin' a shiny white skin instead o' a nice dark color," Paddy added with a sigh.

"I saw you in the fog, you and the girl. You both had your eyes closed." Nefra looked at them, smiling. Paddy's eyes widened, then narrowed as he muttered "Nice, dark color, indeed. Good for sneakin' up on little girls and takin' gold.. "

"Paddy, I'm not forgetting you. We'll talk to Nefra about the gold. It's not going anywhere right away." Stanley grinned at the leprechaun, who still looked unhappy.

Molly said, "Nefra, I'm so glad that we met. But now what do we do about you? You're all alone here, and Stanley has been taken from Ellesyndria ... "

The white dragon looked into Nefra's yellow eyes. "You shouldn't be here, Nefra. You should be with the dragons in Ellesyndria. Morubek would have wanted it that way, no matter how much he cared for you here."

Then he looked at Paddy and Molly. "And I shouldn't be here, either."

chapter sixteen

The Reluctant Tourist

We can't leave now! I've got too much to do, and — and — I just can't go right now! Please, Aunt Shannon!"

Shannon O'Malley took in her niece's tirade with the practiced ease of a born manager. "There's no use talkin' about it, dear, I've taken the time off, and I promised ya a long holiday. Ya were lookin' forward to this not so long ago! Pack enough t'ings for about a week. Tomorrow we'll be out just for the day, but we'll be going south after that, and we will stay over along the way."

Molly stamped her foot. "But things have changed! I have to be here! You just don't understand ... " Her voice trailed off as she marched toward the back door.

"Where do ya t'ink you're goin?"

Molly turned around with a resigned huff. "I have to cool off. I'll be back in just a while, I promise."

Shannon looked at her for a few seconds. "I suppose, but take some water with ya, at least. I'm leaving for Mrs.

Walsh's, but I don't have to be at the pub tonight. Try to be back about half one."

Molly climbed the Burren hills toward the pothole. As she got closer, she tapped her bracelet impatiently, muttering "Paddy, I need to see you. Please hurry."

She arrived at the pothole and looked around. "Where is that leprechaun?" she grumbled.

"Wondering what's got ye in a bad mood!" cried a head as it exploded through the heather covering the pothole.

"Omi ... Paddy! You scared me!" Molly sat down to catch her breath. "Don't ever do that again!"

"The heather's growin' back nicely after Nefra singed it, isn't it?" Paddy chuckled, pulling the rest of him out of the pothole. He brushed stray pieces of the heather from his leather apron. "Now, what's got ye so upset?"

Molly's green eyes glared at the little elf. "We have two dragons that shouldn't be here. We still need to get the gold back to the leprechauns. And my aunt is taking me away on a vacation for a week, and I can't stop her!"

"Aye, your aunt's not one I'd argue with, even if she wasn't three times me size."

"Paddy, I'm needed here! We have to decide what to do!"

He held the heather back with his hand. "Then let's have a meetin'. It's not just you and me anymore. Did ye bring your torch, now?'

Molly raised her hand holding the flashlight in mute response. Clicking it on, she descended into the pothole, Paddy following.

Soon they reached the ledge in the cave's large chamber, Nefra's place, as Paddy was now calling it. "Hello, Molly, Paddy," Stanley's cheerful voice rang out. "Nefra, would you do the honors?"

A bright stream of flame erupted in the blackness, sweeping the walls briefly. It ignited three torches that had been attached to the cave walls. The torchlight proved sufficient to see by.

"T'ought it would save your batteries," Paddy beamed.

"Thanks, Paddy," Molly said as she switched her flashlight off. "Hi, guys. Is everything all right for you?"

"All is well." Nefra's strange voice still echoed inside Molly's head. "We have been talking about the gold. The leprechauns are not men, so I will return the gold to them." She looked longingly at Stanley. "Even though I like it very much."

Stanley shook his head. "You need friends for a change, Nefra. Keeping the gold will make new enemies. You are wise to return the gold."

"I am not so wise. You are persuasive." Nefra murmured, but the look she gave the larger dragon said that she didn't mind.

"What's going on with those two?" Molly whispered to Paddy.

"Careful, those ears of Stanley's can pick up a hummingbird's wings at a hundred yards." Paddy replied. A pointed wink from a violet eye confirmed Paddy's statement. Raising his voice, Paddy continued, "Molly's aunt wants to take her on holiday. She'll be gone for a week."

The dragons exchanged glances. "That might work out all right," Stanley said. "We're not planning on moving the gold until the new moon, when it's darker. That's ten days from now. We'll just stay put here until then, except for fishing excursions."

"Yes," Nefra's voice resonated inside Molly's head. "You should go for a while. We can make the preparations. I think it will be better this way."

"Doesn't anybody want me around?" Molly asked shrilly.

"Molly." Nefra's voice echoed in her skull. The black dragon's yellow eyes were squarely on the distraught girl. "I ask you to trust me in this. It will be ... *safer* if you are away for a while. All will be well. You will understand later."

"Safer? Are you saying you're dangerous?"

"Not in the way that you think."

Molly felt goose bumps rise on her arms. "I don't know if that makes me feel better or not."

"Well, it looked like a nice day outside," Paddy offered. "You'll have a fine trip with your aunt if th' weather holds."

"I know," Molly sighed. "Aunt Shannon is only trying to get my mind off of mom and dad. I wish that I ... "

"*Molly!*" Paddy cried sharply.

"Oh!" Molly covered her mouth. "I'm sorry, Paddy, I almost forgot! If you hadn't yelled at me, I would have ... "

Paddy grasped her hand. "It's all right, girl. I don't think ye would have been th' first to use a wish unt'inkingly. But there's a lot at stake here." He smiled up at her. "At least we know what you're t'inkin' about."

Molly nodded. "I'll be careful. You won't be with us on this trip, so I'll have to be."

———

The next morning was a nice day, as Paddy had hoped. Molly and her aunt drove the few miles to Doolin and parked at the pier. Shannon went to get the ferry tickets while Molly looked across the water toward the Aran Islands.

Surrounding the concrete dock and the launching ramp for smaller boats, the shoreline looked very much like the Burren near Murroogh. The rocks looked like they had been split apart into great stones, leaving deep fissures between them, yet the tops were almost flat and even so that you could step or hop from one to the next.

"Aunt Shannon?" Molly asked as her aunt returned. "These rocks look a lot like the rocks in the Burren."

"This is the Burren, dear. Doolin is about the furthest part of the Burren, on the southwest corner, but it's the Burren just the same. The rocks on the Arans look this way, too. The same type of land runs out to sea to make up the islands."

"Did you get the tickets?"

"Indeed I did. Now we just wait for the ferry to come in. Is that it now?"

Molly peered across the choppy water. She could make out something white moving across the water, just coming around Inisheer. If it hadn't been on the water, she couldn't have been sure it was a boat at that distance.

"It'll be about twenty minutes before it's here. It's bringing people over who spent the night on one of the islands."

The sun had risen well above the green hills behind them before the trim white boat pulled up to the pier. Its motors churned as it pushed the boat against the concrete, cushioned by rubber boat bumpers let down over the side on ropes. The crew slid an aluminum walkway into place, and the overnight passengers began leaving the boat.

After handing their tickets to the man at the walkway, Molly and her aunt boarded and climbed down a steep, narrow staircase to the lower deck at the back of the ship. A fairly large seating area lay forward from there, with padded bench seats enough to hold about a hundred people. The O'Malleys found a place near the back so they could get out quickly when they arrived on Inishmore.

When it seemed as if the room could hold no more, the boat's engines roared louder and it began to float backwards. Men pulled the thick mooring ropes aboard, and hauled the boat bumpers back in to use at their next landing. After pulling clear of the dock, the boat changed directions and lurched forward. Molly could see the white-tipped waves rolling in every direction. Soon their speed picked up and the Doolin dock began to shrink in the distance.

"Look now, Molly! It's a grand site aft!"

"Aft?"

"Aft is the rear of the boat, dear. Ya see Doolin in the middle of the coast there? To the right ya can see the Cliffs of Moher. We'll see them up closer later today, but ya can see them all at once from here, from O'Brien's castle to Hag's Head!" Shannon pointed to two tiny dots sitting on top of the hills, with a long, dark row of cliffs between them. Hag's Head crested the far south cliff face to her right, guarding the point where Liscannor Bay led into the town of Lahinch.

"Now look to the left, Molly. Do ya see anything familiar?"

Molly immediately recognized the comforting sight of the Burren hill that sloped down to Black Head at the northwest corner of County Clare. Murroogh nestled in the hill's shadow just south of Black Head. "Yes," she murmured, "you don't have to get too far from land to see everything along here, do you?"

The shore continued to slowly retreat as the boat fought its way through the water toward the Aran Islands. Molly returned to her seat in the back. After another ten minutes the boat started making a very load noise in the back. Molly wondered if the engines were all right. Could they explode?

Shannon suddenly appeared beside her, her blue eyes shining. "Molly, come to the aft deck! Hurry!"

Molly followed her aunt outside. She stopped with her mouth hanging open, looking up at a helicopter hovering just behind the boat. "So that's what's making the racket! But what is it doing here? Is the boat sinking?"

A man appeared at the open door of the helicopter. He wore a helmet and a brightly colored jumpsuit. As he dropped from the helicopter, Molly could see a cable that attached to the harness he wore.

Now she could make out the letters on the bottom of the helicopter. "Irish Coast Guard?" she wondered. The man dropped lower and lower, getting closer with each second. Molly knew what was going to happen next, but she was still surprised when he actually stepped onto the small deck on the back of the boat. He unhooked the cable and waved to the helicopter.

"Exciting, isn't it?" Shannon shouted over the roar of the rescue helicopter. "The Coast Guard practices landing on a moving boat every day the weather allows. It helps them prepare for a real emergency. Plus the tourists love it! It's like a free show in addition to the ferry ride, and great publicity for the Coast Guard!"

Molly nodded as the Coast Guard man talked to the crew and some of the passengers for a few minutes. Then the cable was lowered once more. He hooked up and was hoisted up into the air to the helicopter. As the aircraft turned back toward the coast the normal roar of the boat's engines could once again be heard.

Inisheer, the smallest of the Aran Islands was their first stop. A ruined castle tower and stone house dominated the hilltop. Soon they were on their way again, churning through the waves around the middle island, Inishmaan toward the big island, Inishmore.

Passing a lighthouse that stood on a smaller island in the channel, the boat put in to the dock at Inishmore. The crew bustled to put everything in place so that the passengers could disembark.

Molly thought that everyone knew what they were doing except her as crowds pushed past her on all sides. Already some people were wheeling bicycles from the rental shop to the road. Others were making their way to several buses that were lined up close by.

Aunt Shannon's firm tug on her jacket sleeve interrupted her thoughts. "This way, dear. We don't have all day, do we?"

As they walked down the dock toward the nearby buildings, a tall man wearing a maroon sweater and a tweed cap walked up to them. "Pardon me, ladies, but would ye be lookin' for a pony cart ride today?"

Shannon stopped. "We might be. What are your rates, now?" She and the man discussed the details for a couple of minutes while Molly looked around the bustling walkway. Next to the railing that overlooked the harbor stood a pony with large, heavy hooves covered with long hair. The pony stood patiently in harness, hooked to a small two-wheeled green cart. Seats covered in red vinyl provided narrow benches, while a small door in the back allowed one to climb into the cart.

"Molly," her aunt said, "We're going to take a pony cart up to Dun Anghus. Hop in, it takes a while to get there."

The tall man led them to the pony cart that Molly had been looking at. He opened the back door and Molly and her aunt found seats on one side. The man sat on the other side.

"This is Patrick. He lives on the island." Shannon pulled her jacket around her. "It's a bit breezy today, but it should be nice."

"Where did you say we were going?" asked Molly.

"Up to the fort, Dun Anghus." Patrick flicked the pony's rump lightly with his crop. "Whueh, whueh," he urged, and the pony started down the crowded road.

"A fort? Like a ringfort?" Molly asked.

"Yeah, only it's a half-ringfort." Patrick answered their questions readily, but Molly had the feeling that he was a quiet man, rarely speaking outside of his days driving the pony cart unless necessary. She wondered if all of the islanders gave the impression of having lived there forever.

"It's about a half hour ride. Then ye can go up to the fort and look around for about an hour. I can pick ye up about one."

"That should leave us enough time," Shannon nodded.

The cart squeaked as it rolled past the many visitors walking along the road. An occasional bus squeezed past with its load of tourists crammed into the seats. The pony cart allowed a wonderful view in all directions of the island, and was quiet except for the clip-clop of the pony's hoofs on the asphalt road.

"This is so nice," sighed Shannon with satisfaction. "It's grand to be out in the open air, and it's faster than walking. The buses are even faster, but ya don't get the view."

Soon the buses were far ahead of them, and the walkers were left behind. Once in a while a bicycle would roll past, its rider pedaling hard to climb the steady grade leading ever higher toward the fort.

Molly could see a high point ahead on the hills. A pathway was visible even from this far away. "Do you take us all the way to the fort?" she asked.

"I can only take ye as far as the entrance. Ye have to walk up from there. It's about twenty minutes."

They reached the endpoint of their ride, marked by the many empty pony carts parked by the side of the road. The drivers stood in small groups talking to each other. Molly thought that Patrick would be joining them soon while he waited for the O'Malleys to return from Dun Anghus.

"Where's the fort from here?" Molly asked her aunt.

"Up on top of that hill," Shannon replied, pointing.

It looked like it was a long way up, but it was nothing Molly hadn't done before. She wondered how secret her hikes into the Burren were. Aunt Shannon had been pretty casual about it the last time Molly went up there.

They passed through the visitor center and started on the pathway to the ancient fort. The path was made out of rocks laid fairly flat, with stone walls flanking each side. Many people were walking on the path, and it was wide enough to allow traffic in both directions.

It took about twenty minutes, as Patrick had said, to reach the summit. An outer wall of stones piled some twelve feet high had a doorway made in it. The train of visitors had to slow down and climb single file through the opening to enter the inner circle of Dun Anghus.

"Stay close to me, Molly." Aunt Shannon warned.

"Why?"

"Hmmm ... I think the best way to explain it to ya is to show you. Come with me."

The two walked toward the side where there was no wall. Shannon grasped Molly's hand firmly as they approached. "Oh," gasped Molly. "I understand."

There was no wall because there was no need to protect this side from attack. The semi-circle enclosed by the walls ended at the edge of a sheer cliff that stood hundreds of feet above the white foaming water below.

"Awesome!" Molly looked along the coastline in both directions. From this height she could see cliffs all along the western shoreline of Inishmore. Several inlets looked particularly dangerous as the water crashed against the cliff base. All around lay the familiar broken rock of the Burren, with green plants growing in the gaps.

Inside the fort, much of the space had been taken over by grass. Molly supposed the grass was there because the stones had all been dug up to build the massive walls. Many small flowers grew readily on the green carpet.

A half hour later Shannon said, "Molly, I hate to rush ya, but we need to leave now to catch our pony cart back to the harbor."

Molly nodded. "That's all right. We've seen most of it. This is really neat!"

The views were equally beautiful as they began their descent from the fort. The island of Inishmore lay stretched out before them, with gray limestone slabs dominating the hillsides. Walls of stone ran everywhere, and beyond everything was the water.

Patrick was waiting for them patiently where he had dropped them off. "Didja have a good time, then?" he asked.

Molly nodded as she climbed into the cart. "It was really cool. Are there cliffs everywhere in Ireland?"

"Much of the coastline is cliffs, yeah," he replied. "I'll take ye back down the coast road. It's a bit longer, but it's flatter and ye can see the other side of the island."

On the way back Molly was impressed by the number of stone walls dividing the land into small areas. "How old are the walls?" she asked.

"Oh, several hundred years at least. There's no place else on earth that ye could build the walls we have, for there's no shortage of building material here in Eire. Some of the younger men have started businesses building new stone walls, they're very popular now."

"Have you ever built stone walls?" Molly's eyes were wide.

"Aye. It's back-breakin' work, I'll tell ye."

A beautiful bay pressed into the island's east coastline. The pony cart bumped steadily around it on the road, coming at last to the small harbor area. Shannon paid the driver for his services, adding a tip as well. "T'ank ya for the wonderful time! We enjoyed the trip so much!"

"Are ya hungry now?" Shannon asked her niece. "We've certainly been hiking long enough to work up an appetite."

"Oh, yes. My stomach has been growling for a while now."

"Let's try this restaurant here. It looks nice enough."

The restaurant was nice, and fairly new. They ordered sandwiches and orange soda.

"Aunt Shannon, has my dad said anything about how mom is doing? I haven't heard from him in ages. I'm worried."

Shannon dabbed her lips with her napkin. "I know, dear. I'm sure if anyt'ing serious were happening, he'd give us a ring. No news is probably good news, but I imagine it's drivin' ya crazy."

"That's for sure," Molly sighed. "I w– " She quickly cut off her sentence and took another bite of her sandwich.

"You what, dear?"

"Nothing." Molly swallowed and took a sip of her soda.

"Molly, your hand's positively trembling! What on earth is wrong?"

So close, Molly thought. *I was so close to saying the third wish out loud. I've really got to be careful.*

She took a deep breath. "I'll be all right, Aunt Shannon. I'm just worried about stuff, that's all."

Shannon smiled at the red-haired girl, but a trace of worry remained in her own eyes. "I know, dear, it's rough at your age anyway. All of this business with your family... " She reached over the table and laid her hand on top of Molly's. "T'ings will work out eventually."

Molly returned the smile. "Yeah, but there is so much stuff to work out."

After lunch they went to one of the sweater shops by the dock. Molly and Shannon each picked out a beautiful cable-knit sweater to take home. "These are wonderful patterns, aren't they?" Shannon asked. "Most people don't know that they have only been making sweaters on the Aran Islands since the 1930's. Since then their patterns and quality have become famous all over the world. It's really helped the economy. Life was very hard here."

The afternoon was nearly gone, so they gathered at the dock with the other passengers returning on the ferry to Doolin. They found seats inside the boat and stayed there for the trip. An hour and a half later, they stepped off the walkway onto the Doolin pier.

"Let's grab dinner at the pub. Then we still have the Cliffs of Moher to see before they close." Shannon fired up the little car's motor and they traveled the short distance to Fisher Street and O'Conner's Pub.

"Hello, Shannon! I t'ought T'ursday was yer day off this week!" The bartender boomed as they walked past the dark wooden bar.

"It is, Michael, but I brought my niece in to sample your cookin' tonight! What's the special?"

"Atlantic salmon, served wit' a cream sauce, fresh veggies and three scoops of the best mashed in Clare!"

"We'd better have two, then, with some hot tea. And try not to beat us to our table."

"You'd best hurry, then," Michael smiled as he retreated into the kitchen.

"Let's sit over here," Shannon whispered. "And I'm not kidding about the food getting to the table before we do."

They were barely seated when two steaming platters were slid in front of them. Molly's mouth watered, it looked delicious. And it tasted even better.

Molly managed to eat most of her dinner. "No need for a box, we're going to be on the road for the next five days," Shannon said cheerily. "I'm lookin' forward to this holiday, aren't you, Molly?"

Molly smiled, trying to look cheerful. "Well, we've avoided disaster so far." She wondered what the dragons and Paddy were up to. Ooh! It was so frustrating not knowing. "Let's go see the Cliffs of Moher."

The drive to the Cliffs was surprisingly short. "It's only about six kilometers," Shannon said as they pulled into the gravel parking lot. "You've seen some cliffs today, but none quite like these."

They walked across the road to the entrance. A modern visitor's center had been dug out of the hillside, with large curved windows to let light inside. "There's the path up to O'Brien's castle," Shannon pointed to the right. "But first come this way," and she led Molly straight ahead.

Climbing a short rise, Molly caught her breath. A giant row of four massive cliffs jutted out into the ocean. As they receded into the distance, the perspective made them appear smaller. She had seen them from the ferry at a great distance, but up close they were spectacular.

The second cliff had a dark spot on it close to the water. She looked at it more intently and gasped. A huge cave! That must be the cave where Nefra lived for several years, before the visitors coming to see the Cliffs made it too difficult to stay hidden. She shivered with delight, feeling the excitement of seeing history unfold right in front of her.

"D'ya like it, dear? Let's go up to O'Brien's castle, now. There's still a good view of the Arans, or at least Inisheer from there, and ya have a different look at the south Cliffs."

Shannon was exuberant, looking around at the scenery with her face beaming. "We'll take a picture when we come back down with the Cliffs behind ya."

O'Brien's castle was a round gray tower, impressive in stone but not particularly tall to Molly's mind. "When was this built?" she asked.

"In the 1830's, I think," Shannon replied. "One of the O'Briens wanted to make the land more attractive to tourists. He had a vision of attracting tourists to Ireland and to this area in particular. Many people were coming to see the Cliffs even then, and he wanted to take advantage of that. He was definitely a man ahead of his time."

Shannon took Molly's picture in front of the Cliffs just before sunset. She asked a middle-aged couple if they would take a picture of Shannon and Molly together. Molly thought about the Cliffs glowing in the sunset all the way back to Murroogh.

chapter seventeen

That Olde Irish Magic

Late the next morning they left again, this time headed for Bunratty. Bunratty was only a couple of hours drive from Murroogh, and a few minutes from Shannon Airport.

Turning off the highway, a castle appeared abruptly on their left side. Shannon followed the road around the corner of the castle. Beyond a narrow bridge was a parking lot clearly labeled "Bunratty Folk Park." They parked the car and walked under a large green awning to the entrance.

When Shannon Airport was built, many of the old cottages and houses were going to be destroyed. Instead several of the best examples were moved to the grounds surrounding nearby Bunratty Castle to create the Folk Park.

Shannon and Molly walked through the Folk Park looking at the cottages with thatched roofs, chickens freely roaming the grounds, and houses where staff sliced up fresh apples for the dessert at the nightly evening feasts. An old stone chapel graced a meadow not far from a working mill where a water wheel circled continuously, filling the air with a comforting splashing sound.

Closer to the castle, a village area had been constructed with buildings set close together. Shops held all kinds of souvenirs and Irish memorabilia for those who wanted them.

The castle itself was imposing, its weathered gray stones towering over the rest of the park. Molly and Shannon climbed the narrow spiral staircase, cut from limestone, to reach the top of the tower.

From the top they had a beautiful view in all directions. They could look down directly on the roof of Durty Nellie's, a pub across the street that had been in business since 1620.

A mural on the castle wall told the story of the castle. Bunratty Castle was built originally starting in the 13th Century, beginning with a wooden structure that was transformed into a Norman walled fortress. It was brought to its present design in the middle 15th Century, with four towers, a great hall, and several rooms. It was largely destroyed in the 17th Century by the Cromwellian wars, but beautifully restored in 1960.

Later that evening, the O'Malleys made their way to the traditional Irish folk night. With about 150 other people, they sat at tables in a large room with a stage. Actors presented the program for the night, which included playing traditional Irish tunes on fiddles, concertinas, guitars, and tambourines. The entertainment featured Irish dances, singing and story telling as well. Between show segments the actors served as waiters, serving a traditional Irish meal, with Irish stew, salad, dessert, brown bread, and a variety of drinks.

Molly enjoyed the evening, especially the sing-a-long where everyone sang an old Irish song. The words had been printed out for the guests, so you just had to learn the tune.

"Thanks, Aunt Shannon," Molly said as they pulled into the parking lot at the bed and breakfast Shannon had reserved for the night. "I enjoyed learning about the castles, and how people lived, and all of the cool music and food and stuff."

Shannon laid a hand gently on Molly's head. "I hoped ya would like it, dear. Ya were so alone when you first came, and I wanted to help ya not be bored, as ya said." She pursed her lips briefly. "Then ya started to worry about your parents, Lord knows who wouldn't, and started this talk about leprechauns and the lot..." Shannon's eyes filled with tears. "I was worried about ya, Molly. But ya seem to handle yourself well goin' off into the Burren, though I'm not completely comfortable when ya do. And ya haven't told me any more stories about leprechauns and dragons for a while."

Molly looked sadly into her aunt's eyes. "And what if I did?"

Shannon exhaled. "Whew! I guess I would chalk it up to an overactive imagination, brought on by the stress of your family situation." She looked uneasily at the girl in the seat beside her. "Do ya ... have more stories about leprechauns and dragons?"

"Nothing that you could remotely believe."

Shannon nodded. "Alright, then. It's late, and we have a drive ahead of us tomorrow down to Blarney. Let's go in and get a good night's rest."

They were blessed with another good day as they drove south. "Maybe it's making up for all of the rain the first two weeks I was here," Molly grumbled.

"It's grand weather for this time of year, not too hot," Shannon laughed. "First stop today is Adare. It's just a half hour or so away."

Adare was a small town, where a row of thatched roof houses greeted them. The thatched houses seemed to have all been acquired by various businesses, including restaurants and clothing stores.

"Let's go to the visitor center, across the street," Shannon suggested. "We'll see what is going on today."

At the information desk they picked up a map of the attractions in Adare. There was a castle nearby that they had seen coming into the town. Since they had already seen Bunratty Castle, they decided not to tour another right now.

"What's this?" Molly asked, pointing to a black box on the map.

"It says it's a friary," Shannon replied. "Let me ask about it."

After a short conversation with the person at the help desk, Shannon turned back to Molly. "She says that it's an old friary that's in ruins now. There's also an old church, also in ruins. The good news is that they both sit on the golf course grounds, and there is no admission charge! We can just walk right out and see them."

The drive to the golf course was brief, only a half mile or so. Shannon checked with the staff to make sure it was alright to walk out on the course, and they assured her that it was. Within a few minutes Shannon and Molly were strolling along the path leading to the greens.

"Oh, look, Aunt Shannon!" Molly pointed to the right immediately.

"The old church cemetery, I would say. It has Irish high crosses on the tombstones and everything." Beyond the cemetery lay the walls of the old church. The roof was long since gone.

Continuing around the course, more ruins came into view. "That must be the friary," Shannon mused. "It's pretty good sized."

A single tower rose over the walls that stretched for over a hundred feet. Molly found an entrance past the first wall and stopped just inside.

"Cool," she whispered. "Aunt Shannon! You've got to see this!"

The walls formed a large courtyard within the friary. But within the courtyard lay another courtyard wall, tucked inside the first. The second wall held an entire row of Gothic arch windows, carved from stone and recessed into the wall with amazing workmanship. Across the courtyard, the opposite inner wall displayed a row of miniature columns set in rounded Roman style arches.

"Look at all of the moss growing here on the rocks. I wonder how much sun gets in here?" Molly touched the spongy moss.

"Molly, this is really nice," Shannon agreed. "Let's see what's on the other side."

Beyond the tower was the main room of the friary, adorned by a single large gothic window with several arches crisscrossing it to form a delicate framework. It was made all of stone.

They walked back to the car, watching for golfers so they wouldn't get smacked by a stray golf ball. "Ireland has a lot of ruins from a long time ago, don't they?" Molly asked.

"Oh, my, yes. Not just Middle Ages stuff like this friary or all of the old castles. Remember Dun Anghus that we saw the day before yesterday? There're places even older than that."

After a quick lunch in Adare they drove south again for another hour and a half. Shannon located their bed and breakfast in Blarney before they took their excursion to Blarney Castle.

"Why are we going to Blarney Castle, Aunt Shannon? We didn't go to the castle in Adare."

"Well, that's a grand question. I suppose it's a matter of tradition. You've not heard of the Blarney Stone, then?"

Molly shook her head.

"There're a number of stories about where it came from. There was a stone, named the Stone of Scone, which was used in Scotland. When a new king or queen of Scotland was crowned, they sat on the stone."

"What's so special about it?"

"The most popular story is that it was Jacob's pillow. D'ya know that story? Jacob was the son of the patriarch Isaac and the grandson of Abraham. He was at a turning point in his life – his brother Esau was mad at him, and he wasn't sure where he stood with his father. He decided to go back to his mother's ancestral home and get a wife for himself. When he stopped for the night, he used a stone for his pillow. That very night, Jacob had a vision. He saw a ladder that went up from the earth all the way to heaven, and the bottom of the ladder was the place where his pillow lay. Angels went up and down the ladder between heaven and earth. God told Jacob that he would be blessed, and that a mighty nation would come from his family. When Jacob woke up, he felt that the place must be the gateway to heaven. He took the stone he had used for his pillow and made a pillar."

"That happened over in the Holy Land. How did the stone get to Ireland?"

"The story goes that the prophet Jeremiah brought the stone to Ireland. It was later taken to Scotland, where the Scottish kings sat on the stone when they were crowned. There it became known as the Stone of Scone. In the early 14th Century, Robert the Bruce cut the stone in two and gave half to Cormac McCarthy for helping Robert in a battle. McCarthy set the stone in the tower of Blarney Castle. That's where it got the name "Blarney Stone." The rest of the Stone of Scone was later taken by the English, who built it into an ornate throne-chair, and they have crowned all of *their* kings and queens sitting on that chair – and on the stone – since that time."

"So why are we going to see an old stone?"

"D'ya know what the word 'blarney' means?"

"Not really."

"Queen Elizabeth I, who ruled England, wanted the Irish chiefs to acknowledge her as the rightful ruler of Ireland. Cormac Teige McCarthy, the Lord of Blarney, was very diplomatic in answering the Queen's requests. He promised loyalty to the Queen without actually giving up anything. This made Queen Elizabeth very frustrated, and she complained to her advisors that McCarthy was giving her "a lot of Blarney." That's how the word 'blarney' originated. It means to speak eloquently about a subject without ever really saying anything."

"Okay... so what does that have to do with the Blarney Stone?"

"The legend grew up that whoever would kiss the Blarney Stone would gain the gift of eloquence in their speech, or more simply, the gift of gab. Many people visit Blarney Castle each year to kiss the Stone. It's one of the best-known Irish traditions."

"I see... kind of a magic stone."

"Ya could say that."

They pulled into Blarney Village and followed the signs to the castle grounds. Shannon bought their tickets. Once inside, a path led alongside a stream toward the castle. Shannon said "There's only one tower remaining of the castle; so many castles were destroyed by wars over time. But this last remaining tower is the one with the Stone in it."

Towering above the lush green grass and clover of the grounds, Blarney Castle looked impressive even in ruin. A massive foundation could be seen at the base, and four sides of smooth rock climbed high above its surroundings. A pair of round watchtowers guarded the entrance, but they stopped far below the top of the Blarney tower.

"They put the Stone all the way at the top of the tower," Shannon winked. "Are ya ready for a climb?"

"The top of that?" Molly moaned. "It better be worth it."

Much like Bunratty Castle, spiral stairs made from stone wound around inside the corner of the tower, allowing you to climb up. The staircase at Blarney was much narrower than the one at Bunratty, however. Molly was glad she was small, as it made it much easier to climb. Thin, tall windows cut through the walls gave them their only glimpses of the outside and a sense of how high they were.

When they reached the top, a line of people stood around the edge of the tower to their right. The middle of the tower was open, so that it could be described as hollow. Across the open space, on the other side, the line of people stopped facing a man in a red jacket kneeling down. The next person in line would lie down on his or her back, then they would get back up and walk away to the left. An official photographer stood close by taking pictures of everyone as they lay down.

"What are they doing over there?" Molly pointed.

"They're kissin' the Blarney Stone. The stone is set below the wall, so it's several feet lower than the walkway. To kiss it, ya have to lie down on your back, and bend down backwards to kiss the stone while you're upside down."

Molly stared at her aunt. "You're kidding."

"Not a bit, dear. You'll get a better look when ya get up there. The man in the red jacket, he holds ya to make sure ya don't fall. And they've put up iron rails ya can hold onta, to make it easier. I'll take your picture if you take mine – alright?"

Molly was unsure about kissing the Blarney Stone as the line moved slowly around the tower perimeter. She looked over the edge to take her mind off of it.

The view was wonderful from the top. Much green space had been acquired around the castle, and the city had not allowed a lot of building close to the grounds.

"This is beautiful, it's so green. I wonder if Ellesyndria is like this." Molly thought of the dragons sitting in the dark cave all day, while she enjoyed the sights of Ireland. She still wanted to help. But she wanted to help her own family, too. If only she could use her third wish to...

"What is Ellesyndria?" Shannon was smiling at her.

"What? Oh, just a place that I heard about. You know, one of those fairy tale kinds of places."

"It must be beautiful if this reminds ya of it. Oh, look, it's almost our turn. Watch the person in front of us, so ya can see how to do it. Ya won't be able to watch me since you'll be snapping my picture."

Molly watched carefully, then it was her turn. "Lie down on your back, here, ma'am," the man in the red jacket said quickly. She did so. "Now grab the iron bars, and lean down." Molly noticed that the person in front of her had leaned back to kiss the rock where it was a blue-gray color instead of the brownish color above it. She grabbed the bars and pulled herself down quickly to the odd-colored stone. Giving it a quick peck, she pushed herself up, aided by the man in the red jacket.

"Got it!" Shannon said, handing the camera to Molly. "The camera's ready to go. My turn!"

Shannon quickly kissed the stone as Molly caught the event on the camera. They moved on around the wall to allow others to have their chance to gain the gift of gab.

Looking over the wall from this side, Molly could see the entire village below.

"D'ya see that building over there? The one with the rows of white windows? That's Blarney Woolen Mills, a nice shopping mall. We'll go there after we finish here." Shannon pointed it out. "We've got the garden to see first."

After descending the steps on the other side of the tower – Molly thought it was very smart to have one set of steps just for going up and another set of steps just for going down – the two walked to the Rock Close garden.

"Alright, this garden was built in the early 1700's by the owners of the Blarney Castle grounds." Shannon read from a brochure she had picked up at the gate. "Let's see what's in here."

The garden held many interesting things. In one spot, small boulders rested in a circle, overgrown with moss and flowers. A sign identified it as the 'druid circle.' Larger boulders created natural walls and mazes throughout the garden.

One of the most interesting sites was the 'Witch's Stone." A sign explained the legend of a witch who revealed the secret of the Blarney Stone to McCarthy. For her action, she was entombed in the rock, which now bears her image. She can escape only at night, and must return to the stone at dawn.

"Look at the stone, Aunt Shannon! Here's the witch's nose, and her eye, and her mouth!"

"Yes," agreed Shannon. "I'm glad we won't be here after dark."

It was late in the afternoon when they left the grounds and found a restaurant close by. After dinner they drove to the Blarney Woolen Mills and shopped for several hours. The inside was bright and modern, with areas dedicated to Aran sweaters, jewelry, and Waterford crystal.

"Ready to call it a night?" Shannon asked merrily, a shopping bag in each hand.

"My legs are ready to call it a night. All this walking after climbing to the top of Blarney Castle has done it for me."

It was nice to finally relax at the bed and breakfast after a busy day. Tomorrow would be filled with activity, too, when they would drive around the Ring of Kerry.

That night, Molly fell asleep as soon as her head hit the pillow. In her dreams she saw her parents sitting together, her father home for the evening, and her mother smiling. That and an image of a shamrock glowing green for the last time.

chapter eighteen

An Unlikely Event

Molly could hardly wait for Aunt Shannon to fall asleep. Her aunt did not approve at all of her niece wandering the Burren at night. But it had been eight hours since they had returned home from their long holiday, and Molly was dying to find out what had happened in her absence.

Her fairy boots gripped the rocks securely as she stepped over a grike. As she approached Nefra's place, she rubbed her bracelet gently to let Paddy know she was coming.

Pushing back the concealing heather, she lowered herself into the pothole. "Psst!" came a whisper behind her. Looking around, she saw Paddy scramble up to the opening and drop softly beside her. "Ye could give a leprechaun a wee bit more warnin'," he grinned. "It's grand to see ye, Molly!"

Giving the elf a quick hug, Molly asked "I assume the dragons are still here? What's been going on?"

"Yes, they're here. And a lot's been goin' on, if ye catch me drift."

Molly looked puzzled. "I guess I *don't* catch your drift. What do you mean?"

Paddy rolled his eyes toward the cavern below them. "I think that Nefra is very much taken with young Stanley. Not that I've seen dragon affection before... "

"What!" Molly sat down and stared at Paddy. "They're in love?"

"If not in love, then headin' right for it. They've been rubbin' their necks against each other, sleepin' right next to each other. And Nefra makes those dreamy yellow eyes every time Stanley says somet'in'."

"Well, I suppose they are certainly old enough for that sort of thing. Stanley is 850 years old, and Nefra is ... what, almost 700?"

"690. Both in their prime for dragons."

Molly shook her head. "I'm glad I don't have to worry about that stuff yet. I have enough problems. Let's go see them."

The friends climbed down the tunnel, using Molly's flashlight to guide them. As the tunnel enlarged, the distinctive sound of Nefra's flaming breath echoed against the walls and the torches lit up.

"Hello," Stanley said with a dragon's smile. "We saw you coming."

"I'm glad *you* can see in the dark," Molly replied. "I'm even gladder that you recognized Paddy and me and lit the torches instead of us!"

"Your scent is unique, too," Nefra added, and her voice sounded inside Molly's head. Molly shivered. She had not heard Nefra's voice for a while, and had almost forgotten the strange effect it had on her.

"You're sayin' we smell, then?" Paddy joked.

"Well, the leprechaun more than the girl," Stanley said with a wink.

"How are you two getting along? You're fishing in the Bay for food?" Molly looked at the dragons in the flickering light.

"Nefra is the better fisher," Stanley said. "She keeps us both well fed."

"Stanley is too modest," Nefra added. "He has become a fine fisher in a very short time." Her eyes shone as she looked at the white dragon.

"Ye see?" Paddy whispered to Molly.

Molly nodded. "What are the plans for the gold?"

Stanley coughed, and a small blizzard swirled in the cave air before sinking into the darkness below. "Paddy, I think you need to take this one."

Molly turned to the leprechaun with a questioning look. "Paddy? What is it? What's wrong?"

Paddy sighed and locked his fingers together. "Everyt'in's goin' well. We plan to deliver th' gold to th' leprechauns on th' new moon, five days from now. It'll be at th' dolmen, not too far from here. Stanley and Nefra can fly th' gold using Morubek's cloak, it'll be faster with both o' them workin' together."

"But..."

"But th' leprechauns still don't trust havin' a human around. They don't want ye t'be there, Molly. I can't get 'em t'listen to reason!"

"After all I've done for them! For you!" Molly was livid. "I used wishes to help the leprechauns! I've worked to solve the mystery and helped to find their gold! And now I can't even see them get their gold back? Not even a thank you?"

She almost stood up, but Paddy grabbed her before she could get to her feet. "Th' ceiling, Molly, watch your head."

Molly paused, looking at the little man with a pained expression on her face. "Oh, Paddy, I'm sorry, I don't mean to be mad at you. You're great. It's just so disappointing... "

"There, there, girl," Paddy comforted her as he gently pulled her to a seat again. "We've been talkin' about what we can do. Ye can go to the dolmen and see th' gold there before th' leprechauns gather. But they'll not be havin' ye there when they come. I'm sorry, Molly. Ye know how I feel."

Molly hugged him. "I know," she whispered, wiping a tear from her cheek.

"I think it would be a good idea for you to stay at your aunt's house until the new moon, Molly." Stanley sounded apologetic for interrupting.

"Why?" she asked, turning her head to look at him.

"Because you take a risk every time you come out here, especially at night. If you get caught, you might be really grounded and miss everything on the new moon."

Molly thought about it for a minute, and then nodded. "What time should I come back?"

"About two in the morning. We should have the gold moved by then. Try and take a nap earlier so you can stay awake."

"Okay. I guess that's all I can do." She looked at the dragons again. "Are you two - lonely in here?"

Nefra gazed up at the big white dragon. "Not any more." Her voice echoed inside Molly's head.

"Well, that's not what I meant... I mean, that's good to know, too ... I guess I'd better be going." Molly turned to climb back up the tunnel. "I'll see you in five days!" She whispered fiercely, "Paddy, meet me outside."

A few minutes later Molly helped Paddy climb out of the pothole. "Paddy, you were right! Nefra *does* have a thing for Stanley! Does that make things harder?"

"I don't think so. I've talked with Stanley a few times now, and he doesn't seem to have found his special dragon-lady in Ellesyndria in all o' these years. He seems to be quite content having Nefra around."

"Oh." Molly was silent for a minute. "I wonder if Stanley was the right solution for the black dragon problem in more ways than one."

"A wish is a powerful thing, Molly. Me very first wish spell, and it's beyond my understandin', that's fer sure."

"Well, I'd better be getting home. Take care, Paddy, and send a weasel to my window if you need anything before we see each other again." She grinned.

Paddy pretended to smooth his black hair into place. "I'll send th' finest lookin' weasel in all of Eire, if it comes to that."

Molly giggled. "That's what I love about you! You're always so seeerious." She leaned forward and kissed him on the cheek. "Good night, Paddy."

"Good night, Molly." Paddy watched as she made her way down the hill. "We've had good luck so far. I hope that it holds."

The stars twinkled brightly without the moon in the sky. Molly's flashlight picked out a safe path over the Burren stones as she made her way to the pothole.

"Two in the morning— I've been five days without an update, something better happen tonight!" She yawned. "I'm glad I took that nap yesterday afternoon. Stanley seems to know a lot about what humans need."

She stroked her silver bracelet as she came up the final rise. Suddenly a huge shape blotted out the stars. She gasped and crouched down. Two huge dragons landed with only a muffled sound on either side of her, one white, one black with a blue stripe. A leprechaun wearing his finest greenery sat astride the white dragon.

"You guys scared me!" she scolded.

"Ye t'ink you're scared now?" Paddy grinned. "Do we have a treat planned for you!"

"What do you mean?" she asked slowly.

"Molly, climb up onto my back." Nefra's voice resonated in her brain. The black dragon kneeled down and extended a great foreleg out like a ramp.

"What? You want me to ... no, no way! I can't ride a dragon ... "

"Trust me, Molly." Nefra's yellow eyes burned as she looked at the girl.

"Climb on, Molly," Paddy encouraged her. "It's the only way we can get ye t'the dolmen and back on time."

As if in a trance, Molly stepped over the talons and climbed up the great foreleg to Nefra's back. "There's a hollowed spot just in front of my wings," the voice echoed. "Sit there and hold on to the spike. I will not let you fall or come to harm."

Molly sat down where she was told, making sure her flashlight was stowed securely. "N-now what?" she asked.

"We fly," Stanley said softly.

With a tremendous surge, Nefra pushed off the ground and her wings stretched out to catch the night air. A mighty downward flap thrust them swiftly toward the stars. Molly held tight to the spike, and felt Nefra's body turning, shifting slightly as she flew, as if the dragon could feel Molly on her back and was flying to keep her securely in her seat.

From the corner of her eye, Molly caught a glimpse of the white dragon, matching Nefra's speed with practiced ease. It must be wonderful, Molly thought, for them to be out in the open like this after being cramped in that cavern for days on end.

The Burren raced past under them. Hills that would have taken hours to climb, stone walls that would have slowed her progress to a crawl, vanished under the great wings in seconds. Then Nefra dropped into a terrifying dive. The limestone rocks, dim under the starlight, rushed up at them.

The great black wings opened and they floated for a moment, hanging like a yo-yo at the bottom of its string. The dragons landed side by side with a soft crunch.

A strange pile of stones lay before them. Molly realized she was holding her breath and took in a gasp of the cool summer night air. "Is... is that the dolmen?"

"Aye!" Paddy's voice rang clearly. "And there be gold here as well!"

Molly climbed down from the black dragon. She paused, touching Nefra's great nose as she turned her head to her. "Thank you, Nefra, that was amazing."

"You're welcome." Nefra's breath smelled slightly of sulfur, like the smell a car makes when it gets too hot.

Molly turned to the dolmen. The large top slab balanced on two portal stones, large and mysterious in the dim light. As she walked toward it, something moved in the shadows under the dolmen.

"Paddy?" she said uncertainly over her shoulder.

A match flared in the darkness, lighting the face of a wizened leprechaun with a red beard. He lit his pipe, puffing for a few seconds, then he blew a perfect smoke ring out over the Burren. "It's about time ye showed up, I've been waitin' here for hours."

"Ye knew th' appointed time, Kevin, but it's good t'see ye, truly it is." Paddy was smiling from ear to ear.

Kevin grunted as he stepped out from the cover of the dolmen. "Well, here's the gold, girl. Ye wanted to see it, and a leprechaun to boot. Ye should count yourself fortunate." He grabbed a pinch of his lit tobacco from his pipe and quickly threw it into the dolmen. A light flared brightly, illuminating a large pile of gold. The glow remained for a minute as Molly looked at the treasure.

"Thank you, Kevin," she said. "I thought that none of the leprechauns wanted... "

"I'm only here because of the extraordinary circumstances. You've used a second wish for the little people. That's... " he fumbled for words.

"Incredibly selfless?" said Paddy.

"Generous beyond measure?" suggested Stanley.

Kevin glared at them. "Quite remarkable for a big 'un." He turned to Molly. "I'm grateful to ye for what you've done, and I want to give ye this." He reached inside his vest, pulling out a long, golden chain, and handed it to Molly.

"A gift?" she asked, taking it gently from him.

"A payment for your services," he replied gruffly.

"If it were a gift, it would vanish after he left, isn't that right, Kevin?" Paddy grinned.

"That it might." A glimmer of a smile creased Kevin's face, and then it was gone. "The rest will be here shortly. You'd best be on your way, the lot o' ye."

"Thank you, Kevin," said Molly, "for the – payment."

He nodded curtly and stepped back to the dolmen.

Once again the girl and leprechaun mounted their dragons and launched into the night sky. They soon landed at the pothole.

"Thanks for the wonderful night, guys. Seeing the gold, and Kevin, and ... thank you, Nefra for a ride I'll never forget!" Molly stroked Nefra's head tenderly. "You are so awesome!"

"You are welcome, Molly," the voice whispered inside her.

"And Molly?" Stanley said. She turned to the white dragon. "Paddy has it right. Nefra and I are in love."

chapter nineteen

The Choice

geata rima

"Aunt Shannon? Is there any news from Dad or Mom?" Shannon nodded. "I just got a call from your father, your mom is doing as well as can be expected, he said."

"What does that mean?" Molly groaned. "I need to know what is going on!"

"What that means is that your father is takin' care of your mom, I'm takin' care of you, and you don't have to take care of anyone!" She drew Molly next to her. "Give him a bit more time. Your mom really needed some rest. It takes a while to recover from something like that. Anyway, don't ya enjoy my company, now?"

"Of course I do." Molly kissed her aunt on the head. "I'm just worried that more time isn't fixing it. He had years before to fix things, and things just got worse. How do I know that things are getting better now?"

Shannon sighed. "Ya don't, dear. It's been almost three weeks since we had that lovely holiday together. I'd hoped to take your mind off of these worries."

Molly said nothing. She had at least double the worries that Aunt Shannon knew about. The leprechauns had their gold back, but two live dragons were living in Ireland that didn't belong there, and not knowing how her family was doing was tearing her apart.

She pictured a glowing green shamrock for the thousandth time.

"Whether I want to take care of anyone or not, I don't know who to take care of first. Do you need to get to work?"

Shannon glanced at her watch. "Oh, my, I'd best be gettin' over to Mrs. Walsh's! T'anks, dear. I'll see ya tonight." She walked out the door and drove off.

Molly sat in her chair, deep in thought for an hour. Then she packed a lunch and started for the Burren.

"Paddy, come on out." Molly traced the ivy and moon etched into her bracelet with her finger. "I'm almost to Nefra's place."

She reached the hidden opening without seeing the leprechaun. "I really need to see you now," she muttered.

Molly laid her hand on the rock and jumped with surprise. There lay a fresh-plucked late orchid, creamy white with brilliant pink color inside the petals.

"Thought the orchid might cheer ye up a bit." Paddy sat down beside her. "Came to talk, ye did?"

Molly nodded. "It's really serious, Paddy. Now that the leprechauns have their gold back... they did all get their gold back, didn't they?"

"Aye. Most were in such a rush to find a new hiding place they barely said 'thank ye' at all, so ye didn't miss much. But it all went grand."

"Well, since that problem is solved, I-I've been thinking what to do with the third wish."

"I t'ought that would be plain enough. Stanley and Nefra have each other now, I've never seen two happier dragons. Ye deserve to use th' wish for yourself, to wish for your family situation to get better. T'ink of it as a reward."

"You've never seen any dragons before. Paddy, they don't belong here. And I'm responsible for bringing Stanley here with the second wish. I can't just leave him hanging. He didn't ask for any of this."

Paddy scratched his chin. "How do ye know that it wasn't his destiny to be brought here to meet Nefra? If ye hadn't made th' wish, he would never have met his true love."

"I know, I know ... that's what makes it so hard. I can see reasons both ways. There's not one simple answer that will take care of everything. For every problem that a wish solves, it creates two more!"

"Ahh, Molly." Paddy shook his head. "Much as it pains me, th' wishes are yours to use, not mine. 'Tis a great responsibility that comes with a great gift. I should never have cast that spell."

"Oh, no, Paddy, don't ever think that! So much good has come from the wishes already!" Molly blinked back a tear. "So it's been hard on me. I've had to crawl into dark caves, face fire-breathing dragons, and be insulted by leprechauns. But I've also seen fairies dance under the full moon, flown on a dragon's back over the Burren, and became dear friends with someone I didn't even know existed. I wouldn't trade that for anything! I feel like I've grown up so much in the past two months ... " She covered her face with her hands.

"And ye should be enjoyin' your childhood, instead of dealin' with all o' these grownup decisions! Molly, use the wish for your family and for you! It's you that's needin' support now. You've done enough!"

Molly looked up, her eyes red. "That's why I came here. I need to ask someone else if I've done enough."

Paddy sat down heavily. "The dragons."

Molly sighed. "And a rare white dragon in particular."

They climbed down the tunnel to the cavern. With a *whoosh*, the torches ignited, showing the faint trails of smoke that drifted from Nefra's nose. "Thanks, Nefra!" Molly called out.

"What brings us the pleasure of this visit?" Stanley smiled. Molly and Paddy exchanged glances, unsure of where to start.

Stanley frowned slightly and raised his head higher. "Molly, have you been crying?"

Molly looked across the chasm at Stanley, closed her mouth tightly, and nodded.

"Hmmm. May I inquire what is troubling you? As if I didn't have a pretty good idea already."

"You – you know? How?"

"If I had an unused wish, that would be laying heavy on my mind. I've only known you a few short weeks, but in that time, I think I know what a good, kind heart you have. I also think that something else has been bothering you besides a couple of old dragons.

"Now, I was summoned here by a wish, and I can't fly back there on my own." His violet eyes glittered in the firelight. "Molly O'Malley, what is it going to cost you to help a dragon get home?"

Molly did not respond right away. She brushed a tear away, looked up at the recesses of the cavern, then back at the white dragon.

"I'm not supposed to be here, either." She hugged her knees, her eyes downcast. "My dad was spending a lot of time with his work and not much time with my mom and me. Mom finally got exhausted doing everything herself and had to go to the hospital to rest and get better. When Dad came home to take care of her, he didn't think he had time to take care of Mom, and his job, and me." She looked up again at Stanley. "So he chose to get rid of me. He sent me over here to Ireland to stay with Aunt Shannon, and he didn't even get along with my aunt. Now I don't know how Mom is doing, Dad calls every once in a while to say everything is going fine, but he's always said that everything was fine, even when it wasn't. If I hadn't met Paddy, I think I would have gone crazy."

"So you *do* have a lot on your mind," Stanley said softly. "You have to choose between your family, and two dragons that are out of place. I don't envy you, Molly. That's a hard choice. But it's one that only you can make."

"Stop it! Stop it! Will everyone please stop saying that it's all up to me, that it's my choice?" Molly was close to tears again. "Would someone just tell me what they want me to do?"

"Molly, dear, that's not how wishes work." Paddy offered her a red handkerchief. "It has to be what *you* want to do. You've used th' wishes so far to help th' leprechauns. Now you're free to use th' last wish however ye see fit."

Molly grabbed the handkerchief and wiped her eyes. "Why do you have to be so nice?"

"I'm a leprechaun. It's me job to be unpredictable."

Molly laughed, still dabbing tears. "Does the wish have to be made under a full moon?"

"The wishes started under a full moon. It'd be stylish for the wishes to end under one."

"Then let's get this over with. Everyone meet at midnight in the bowl between the hills. I'll have my decision then." Molly handed the damp red handkerchief back to Paddy.

Stanley wiggled with pleasure and folded his great forelegs under him. "I haven't seen this much excitement since the Crusades!"

The moon floated high over the Burren, casting ghostly shadows where the rocks dared to challenge the generally flat limestone fields. A small, red-headed girl made her way confidently over the broken terrain, skipping over an occasional wide gap. The rounded hills of the Burren surrounded the bowl on three sides. She walked to the center of the bowl and stopped, looking around.

"I'm here, Molly," a subdued voice said. Paddy reclined against a pale boulder, resting on the soft grass that surrounded it. "Th' dragons should be here any minute."

"I hope so," she sighed. "I am so tired."

Molly heard the sound before she saw them, air rushing over leathery wings like wind through the trees just before the storm. She looked up as the dragons hovered in the breeze, then landed with a soft scratching sound next to her, tucking their wings along their sides. Salt water dripped silently off of them, reminders of their swim in the Bay from the underwater cave entrance.

"Great. Everyone is here." Molly took a deep breath. "I thought that wishes would make everything easy. But they don't. Everything that a wish gives me has a price tag that comes with it. This final wish isn't going to be any different."

Stanley looked more mournful than he ever had before. A crystal tear rolled down his cheek and froze when it reached his jaw. Paddy simply looked uncomfortable, knowing as he did that he was responsible for granting Molly the wishes in the first place. Only Nefra seemed at peace, her yellow eyes glowing in the night, steam curling lazily from her nose.

"You all know how much I'd like to help my family. My family is so far out of control that I can't even be with them. Except for Aunt Shannon, that is. She has taken care of me in so many ways this summer. Sometimes I'd like to just make everything perfect and all of the bad things go away."

Molly looked at her friends. "If there's one thing I've learned, it's that good things happen when you help others before trying to get something for yourself. So I've decided to help Stanley and Nefra go home to Ellesyndria."

"No... Molly... " Stanley began.

"You said it yourself. It's my decision, and that's final. Now stay behind me while I make this last wish."

"One moment." Nefra's thoughts burned into Molly's head. "Before you make this wish, I have a gift for you."

Molly turned to the black dragon. "A gift?"

"Take the medallion from around my neck. I won't need it any longer." She lowered her great black neck, the blue stripes running down each side to her head. The medallion dangled from the thin strip of black cloth. Molly fumbled with the knot for a few minutes, but finally it relented and the medallion came free.

Molly stepped back, holding the carved stone disc in her hand. "Thank you, Nefra. I'll always treasure it."

"You're welcome." Molly looked up, shocked. She heard Nefra's voice clear and strong, but for the first time the dragon's thoughts did not echo inside her head.

"How... ?"

"You will understand in time, Molly. Make the wish."

Nodding uncertainly, Molly slipped the medallion into her pocket. She pulled her locket on its chain from under her shirt and opened it. The shamrock lay on top of her mother's picture, her dad watched from the other half of the locket. Molly picked up the shamrock carefully and extended her arm.

"I wish that the dragons, Stanley and Nefra, could go to be with the other dragons in Ellesyndria, and live in peace and happiness!"

For a moment the shamrock did not change, giving the impression that it was thinking about how to fulfill this request. Then the green glow appeared around it, which rocketed away from Molly at incredible speed to a spot fifty yards away. It exploded as it struck the rock, flecks of green breaking apart and bouncing across the Burren. The rocks underneath began to glow green as well.

Like a scene from an old horror movie, the rocks themselves began to stir and move like zombies rising from their crypts. They turned upright or rolled drunkenly across the ground, and began piling themselves upon one another.

Smaller rocks bounced toward the rising mound of rubble, joining the frenzy. Two stacks were visible now, growing about a hundred feet apart. It looked as if all of the rocks on the hillside were lurching toward the twin tornadoes of stone, which writhed and twisted.

Then the rocks themselves began to change. As they reached higher into the night sky, they no longer held the familiar broken outlines of Burren flagstones. Their edges turned sharp and smooth, resembling bricks and cornerstones cut from a quarry by an intelligent hand. Like dominoes dealt at a family game night, they clicked neatly into place and rapidly bridged the gap between the two mounds of stone.

With an understated crunch the stone fingers met in the middle, a hundred feet in the sky, where the top was smooth and finished like a rich man's fireplace mantle. Engraved in the very center across the great arch were these letters:

geata Rima

"It can't be," whispered Stanley.

"Blimey," said Paddy softly.

The stones formed a large, nearly circular opening under the arch. Beyond it laid the wreckage of the Burren hillside, stripped of rock, dark grooves marking the march of the stones.

"The stars!" Nefra cried out.

Through the arch the stars began to waver and blur. One by one, then by handfuls, they dimmed and vanished in a field of bright blue sky that rapidly filled the space between the stone. The hillside sprouted thick stands of green grass where moments before only earthen scars had lay. There were mountains in the distance, purple against the horizon, and forests sprawled across the land. Time itself seemed to stop, and the freshest, sweetest air that Molly thought she had ever smelled wafted over them from the portal.

Except for the gateway within the arch, the Burren around them lay stark and cold, bare in the light of the full moon.

"Stanley, is that really the Arch of Rima?" Molly gulped.

"Aye. A sight I truly never thought I would see again." He turned to the others. "It won't remain long. We must say our goodbyes quickly."

Molly rushed to hug the dragon's gleaming white side, her tears falling without shame. "Oh, Stanley, I'll miss you! I hope you get all the happiness you deserve!"

"It was grand to meetcha, old man," Paddy said with a crooked grin. "T'anks for the ride th' other night."

Now Molly raced to Nefra's neck. "And you, poor dear, you finally have a chance to be with the other dragons! Stanley will take care of you."

"I know." Nefra smiled. "Thank you for bringing us together."

The dragons turned toward the arch. Together they sprang into the air, their wings almost touching. Stanley dived into the arch, with Nefra closely following.

"Thanks for trusting me, Nefra!" Molly shouted.

The black dragon turned for a moment, almost motionless in the night air. "I have always trusted you, Molly." Then she was through the arch, shrinking in the distance as she pursued the ice-dragon.

A harsh grating sound broke the stillness. The stones of the arch began to shift and crumble. The vision of Ellesyndria seen through the arch rippled as if someone had cast a pebble onto its watery reflection, and the stars returned. It now seemed impossible that the great piles of stones could remain upright as they teetered above Molly and Paddy's heads.

The top layers melted away as if they had been made of smoke, and the rest fell with a great crash, surrounded by a bright green glow that raced in every direction from the center. Molly and Paddy jumped for cover, but the green cloud of light swiftly faded into the darkness as it rolled over the Burren hillside. Every stone, every rock, every blade of grass was back in its place as if there had been no magic there tonight.

But Molly would remember.

chapter twenty

Reunion

"There's no tellin' who might have heard that racket," Paddy said. "The wish could have concealed all o' it, but we don't have any way o' knowin' for sure. We'd best get out o' these hills."

Quickly the pair made their way toward Murroogh, Paddy keeping an eye out for a hiding place should someone be coming up to investigate the incredible display just ended. They reached the ridge overlooking the village, but could see no signs of lights or activity approaching them.

"That must have been a powerful wish," Molly breathed softly. "How could anyone not have seen or heard that?"

"That was a powerful feeling behind th' wish, me dear. Ye put aside all o' your concern for your family to help th' dragons. That's what made th' wish so strong." The leprechaun patted her arm gently. "Ye did well, Molly O'Malley."

Molly sighed. "I'm still concerned about my family. I just know that a wish is not going to fix it." She fished in her pocket and pulled out the stone medallion. "This thing is bumping around when I walk. I ought to put it in my backpack."

"Oh, yes," Paddy said, "I almost forgot. Just before th' arch fell down, I grabbed this from where it had fallen. Maybe ye can tie the medallion back onto it." He held out the thin band of black cloth.

Molly looked at it closely. "This isn't regular cloth. It's woven, like a flat braid. Nefra must have been wearing this for centuries."

She stretched it out. "Oh, it's way too long for me to use. This must be ten feet long; it's designed for a dragon's neck, not mine."

"Well, how about th' gold chain that Kevin gave ye? That's the right size, isn't it?"

"Yes, it would be about right. I think I have it here in my backpack." She unzipped the pocket and pulled out the chain. "It's just small enough to fit through the brass ring of the medallion, and the right length for a necklace." Molly slid the chain through the medallion and clasped it around her neck.

"Aye, an object such as that deserves t'be worn. Take good care o' it, Molly."

Molly nodded. She knew that she would treasure it always as a gift from a dear friend.

"I'll keep the black cloth, too. It seems a shame to throw it away. Good night, Paddy."

"Good night, Molly. Get some rest, you've been up too many nights for one your age."

Aunt Shannon was very cheerful the next three days. Molly's spirits were down, as she continued to dwell on her parents' state. Only the memories of the great dragons soaring through the magical arch boosted her mood.

"I need to see Paddy again," she grumbled. She packed a lunch with an extra apple and hiked up to the ringfort. Sitting down on a flat rock, she tapped her bracelet absently. "Hey, Paddy, come and talk with me."

"Aye, but only for a minute." Paddy appeared over the wall and scampered down to her side. "There's a group of hikers comin' in from th' Ballyvaughan side, and they'll be here within a half hour."

"Rats." Molly pulled out the apple and handed it to Paddy.

"Ye spoil me, child. T'ank ye."

"Paddy, do you think that my family will ever be together again the way we were?"

"I can't say, Molly. Miracles happen without wishes, too. Remember how we met and became friends."

"I know. It's been cool learning about Ireland, its history and stories – some of them true ... " she winked at the leprechaun. "And I'm really glad that I was able to help the leprechauns and the dragons. Now, I'm just ready to go back to being plain old Molly O'Malley."

Paddy snorted. "You're not so plain as ye let on, girl. It's not every eleven year old outside of Eire that can speak Irish."

"Speak... What do you mean? I don't speak Irish!"

"C'mon, Molly, except for that first minute when she spoke dragon with Stanley, Nefra didn't speak a word that wasn't in Irish when she was here, and you understood everything she said. I need to go, those hikers are getting close, and there's not much cover on the top o' this hill. G'bye, me dear!"

Before Molly could protest further, Paddy had scrambled over the stone wall and was gone.

Walking along the green road, Molly neared the house. Aunt Shannon's car was in the driveway, along with another car. "Oh, man, I hope she didn't call the police because I wasn't home. I left that note like always, I hope she saw it!"

She walked in the back door and set her backpack on the counter. "Aunt Shannon, I'm back!"

"That's grand, Molly! Would ya come out to the living room, dear?" Aunt Shannon didn't sound cross at all. She sounded almost giggly. Curious, Molly stepped into the living room.

Her parents were sitting on the sofa.

Kate O'Malley looked radiant, her blonde hair brushed back and fastened with a comb. Her blue eyes sparkled, something Molly had not seen there for a long time.

Sean O'Malley sat beside his wife, wearing a casual outfit and a smile. His smile was even more comfortable than his clothes, glowing with the impression that he was very glad to be there.

They were holding hands.

"Mom! Dad! What are you doing here?" Molly flew into their arms, and they both enveloped her.

"Surprised?" her dad laughed as he hugged her. "I only wish we could have been here sooner."

"Oh, Molly, Molly ..." her mother buried her face in Molly's hair.

"It's okay, Mom," Molly sobbed. She raised her tear-stained face and looked at them. "Tell me the truth. Is everything all right?"

Her mom smiled. "Everything's fine, dear, everything's more than fine. Your father has something to say."

Molly's dad said, "I'm so sorry for what I put you and your mother through. My family is the most important thing in the world to me. Not just providing for my family, being *with* my family. I've been so stupid. I've taken a position with my company that will allow me to work in the sales region where we live, so I won't be gone nearly as much. I'll still have a few trips here and there, to keep enough frequent flyer miles so we can come back to Ireland and visit my big sister." He smiled at Shannon, who smiled back. "I understand you two have become quite close."

Molly gave Shannon a hug. "She's the best, Dad. Are you two getting along any better now?"

He grinned. "I think I still have a lot to be forgiven for, but we're talking. We're going to stay for a couple of days, then take you back home, if that's okay with you."

"That would be great!"

They stayed up late into the evening talking. Shannon did not have enough space for all of them, so Molly's parents got a room with Mrs. Walsh at the bed and breakfast. Her mother told her, "Molly, you're all settled in here, there's no sense moving you for a couple of days. We'll see you in the morning."

Late that night after Aunt Shannon had fallen asleep, Molly slipped out and headed for the Burren one last time. She stroked the silver bracelet gently, whispering "Paddy. Please come and meet me."

They met in the wooded area where she made the second wish. The leprechaun stepped out from the shadow of a tree, resplendent in his green finery. "Paddy! Why are you all dressed up?"

He smiled thinly. "It's not every day that friends have to say goodbye."

"How did you know about that?"

"I watched th' house, saw th' cars. And a weasel friend o' mine heard somet'ing from below th' window."

"Very handy, having a talented friend like that." Molly felt the tears welling in her eyes.

"It seems ye didn't need that wish after all," Paddy grinned. "I'm happy for ye, Molly, you've gotten everyt'ing ye wanted."

"Not everything. I'm going to be far away from my best friend."

"I've been t'inkin' about that, too," he frowned. He pulled a simple leather pouch from beneath his jacket. "A parting token. But ye can't open it until you're safe home in Chicago."

"Paddy, this is going to kill me!"

"I mean it, not a peek until you're home!"

"Alright. But I don't have anything for you, Paddy."

He looked at her in amazement. "Girl, how could you possibly give this old leprechaun any greater gift than your friendship? We've had a grand adventure now, somet'in' that people write books about! What you've done will be repeated among th' fairy folk for as long as memory lasts and ballads are told! At least, if this leprechaun has anyt'in' to say about it."

Molly stooped to hug the elf. "And I'm sure you will, Paddy, I'm sure you will!"

chapter twenty-one

The Return

*T*he flight home was a little longer than the flight going to Ireland. Molly's dad explained that was because of the jet stream, sort of a "river" of air high above the earth that moves very fast. "The jet stream generally moves from west to east because of how the Earth rotates," he said. "It can help push a plane flying from America to Europe 100 miles per hour faster, so the trip takes less time. Going back the other way, the pilot stays away from the jet stream to avoid the wind slowing him down, but it takes longer anyway because he doesn't have the extra push to help him fly faster."

"Dad, I'm glad that you know all of this stuff from flying so much. I just want you to know that it's okay because you're flying with us this time, and not telling me about it after you get home." Molly took a sip of her ginger ale.

Her dad smiled. "Believe me, sweetheart, this is much more fun than flying alone. Things are going to be different from now on."

They landed in Chicago shortly after noon. Because Shannon Airport had a United States Customs area before they left, they didn't have to wait through any lines when they landed. After collecting their luggage and stacking it on a large cart, Molly's dad went to get the car while Molly and her mom waited on the sidewalk.

"Mom, do you really think Dad's changed?"

Kate O'Malley smiled. "I really think he has. He's changed his job so he'll be closer to home. And I never thought I would get him to go to Ireland. But he went, and you saw him with Aunt Shannon — he's really making an effort to make things better."

A large SUV pulled up. "You brought the Suburban!" Molly exclaimed.

"And how else were we going to get your entire line of luggage home?" her mom teased. "What do you want for lunch?"

"I know a great Irish pub that's on the way home!" Mr. O'Malley called as he opened the tailgate.

"Promise me you'll take me there some other time, Dad. Right now, a regular cheeseburger and a vanilla shake sound good to me."

Mid-afternoon arrived with sweltering heat as they pulled into their driveway. Molly's dad helped bring in the luggage, and Molly couldn't stop grinning as she carried her smaller totes in behind him. Maybe he *had* changed. She certainly hoped so.

Molly spent the better part of an hour unpacking her suitcases. She tossed her dirty clothes into a basket to take to the laundry room later. It seemed strange to set her toothbrush, hairbrush, and everything else back in the bathroom after being at Aunt Shannon's for so long. "I'm really home," she whispered. "But gosh, what a summer!"

She sat on the edge of her bed to examine her very special treasures from Eire. First she traced the etchings of the silver bracelet with its crescent moon and the ivy twining over the surface. Then she looked at the medallion that Nefra had given her, hanging easily on the gold chain that Kevin the leprechaun had used to "pay" her for her services.

Briefly she unfolded the black cloth that had held the medallion around Nefra's neck for so many years. The weave was still impressive for its detail and precision. Molly folded it back up and put it in her dresser drawer.

Taking off her boots, she set them carefully in her closet. "It's not every girl who has a pair of shoes made by a real leprechaun," she chuckled.

Opening her heart shaped locket, she felt her eyes well up as she looked on the faces of her parents. They were a family again, and Molly knew that she was loved, and that she loved them. Across the pictures lay the shamrock that she had used to make the wishes. It was just a shamrock now, drained of the fairy-magic that had summoned a dragon from another place, and sent two back. The wish magic was not meant to put her family back together again, but it seemed right that the shamrock remain close to her parent's pictures.

Then she remembered the leather pouch that Paddy had given her before she left. "I'm home now, so I can open it!" Laughing with excitement, she pulled it from her suitcase pocket and stretched open the pouch's drawstring top. Reaching in with her fingers she retrieved a single gold coin, its surface engraved with a beautiful woodland scene on one side and a mountain on the other.

"Oh, Paddy," she grinned in mock exasperation. "You know that leprechaun gold always vanishes after being given away." Suddenly she felt like she was floating, and the air turned crisp, smelling of salt.

Looking up, instead of her bedroom window she saw the sun setting across the Bay of Galway, the clouds flecked with pink against the turquoise sky. "Either vanishes or returns to th' leprechaun that gave it, th' legends are a bit muddled about that," said a voice behind her. She whirled to see Paddy Finegan sitting on an ancient tree stump on the rise overlooking the Bay.

"Paddy!" she squealed. "How did you do this?"

"None of my doin', I'll warrant," drolled Paddy with a wink. "Ye know I've never been much good with magic." He offered her a chunk of the cheese he was munching on, which she accepted eagerly.

"Paddy, you know you have to tell me how this thing works." Molly's green eyes bored into him. She bit into the cheese and waited for him to reply.

The leprechaun raised his hands in mock surrender. "All right, then, here's what ye do. When ye pull out th' gold coin and t'ink of ol' Paddy and th' grand Emerald Isle, hold on tight and th' gold will return to me. When you're ready to go back, just slip th' coin back into th' pouch."

"Oh, Paddy, that's wonderful!" She gave the tiny imp a great hug and a kiss. Straightening, she sighed and looked around at the sparkling water and the islands in the distance. "I'd love to stay, but no one knows I've gone, and I need to spend time at home right now." She looked at Paddy with a big smile. "Things are going much better between Mom and Dad, and I should be with them. You won't mind if I pop back later for a visit?"

"Be off with ye, then, ye ungrateful wench!" Paddy growled with a huge grin. "And don't come back until ye can stay a bit!"

"I'll do that," Molly nodded, and opened the purse. She paused with the coin poised just above it, and said happily, "Thank you for the gold, Paddy!" She dropped the coin in, and disappeared in a golden haze that lingered for only a moment.

The leprechaun gazed where she had stood for a few seconds. Then he shook his head and murmured, "No, Molly, *you* are th' gold." He climbed nimbly to his feet, pushed his hat forward, tapped out a quick jig on the old stump, and vanished into the Irish twilight.

the Burren By the Bay

by Susan Porter

In a little seaside village
on the coast of Galway Bay,
there is land of rock and flora
that I'd love to see each day.
And that ocean water draws me near
in a calm and peaceful way,
for I never thought I'd be here
'twixt the Burren and the Bay.

Chorus:
Sing hey-o, hey-o
take me away
say hey-o, hey-o
to the Burren by the Bay.

Well there's plenty enough to do here
if you take your time to see,
from the shores of sand and seaweed
to hilltops, oh so green,
where the roaming cattle meet the sheep
along the stone-built walls.
There's much more here than meets the eye
greater than the seagull's calls.

Chorus:
Sing hey-o, hey-o
take me away
say hey-o, hey-o
to the Burren by the Bay.

Now I wonder what will happen,
if it comes that I can't stay?
I would take the memories with me,
and hope I'll return someday...

Sing hey-o, hey-o
take me away
say hey-o, hey-o
to that beautiful, magical place;
to the Burren by the Bay.

How to Order

from Buried Treasure Publishing

Some of the books offered by Buried Treasure Publishing are available through online outlets such as lulu.com, amazon.com, and barnesandnoble.com.

You may also order books directly from the publisher:

Duane Porter
Buried Treasure Publishing
2813 NW Westbrooke Circle
Blue Springs, MO 64015
(816) 210-4314
email: <u>sales@buriedtreasurepublishing.com</u>

You may photocopy one of the order forms on the next few pages and mail in your order with a check.

If you wish to use a credit card, please visit the publisher web site **www.buriedtreasurepublishing.com**, where a link will be provided to order books at this time. Note that prices from online outlets may differ from prices available directly from the publisher.

Missouri residents please add 6.85% sales tax.

Order Form

		Qty	Total
The Best Ride	$7.95	_____	_____
Charlie and the Chess Set ISBN 978-0-615-14018-6	$11.95	_____	_____
Molly O'Malley and the Leprechaun ISBN 978-0-9800993-0-0	$12.95	_____	_____
Tax (MO residents please add 6.85%)			_____
Shipping: $3 for first item, $1 for each additional item			_____
		Total	_____

❑ **Check Enclosed**

Name: _____

Address: _____

_____

email: _____

Phone: _____

Books by Duane Porter:

The Best Ride

Charlie and the Chess Set

Molly O'Malley and the Leprechaun

Future books by Duane Porter:

Molly O'Malley and the Fairy Queen

Molly O'Malley and the Secret of Achill Island

Stanley, the Little White Dragon

Please visit our web site at

www.buriedtreasurepublishing.com

for more information on books,
authors and illustrators!